The Beach Hut
and other stories

Sian Hughes

Biscuit Publishing

Published 2009 © in Great Britain

Biscuit Publishing Ltd
PO Box 123, Washington
Newcastle upon Tyne
NE37 2YW

www.biscuitpublishing.com

ISBN 978 1 903914 36 6

Cover Photos: Mike Hughes   Front Cover Design: Doig Simmonds
Typesetting/ Cover Design: Colin Mulhern

Acknowlegements. The author and publisher wish to acknowledge with thanks previous publication of the following stories: *Incident on Platform Fifteen* (Cinnamon Press); *Mrs. Pinkney and the Wheelie-Bin* (Carousel); *Mrs. Graebner's Special Instructions* (The New Writer); *The Darras* (Blue Nose Press).

Thanks to my husband Mike, for his unfailing support and encouragement; to my daughters, Penny and Lola; and to the following patient and perceptive friends and colleagues: Ann Schlee, Penelope Bennett and Kerry Beckett; Brigitta Ansdell-Evans, Patience Moberly and Gill Hancock; Edna Wallace, Vivika Mortensen, Branwyn Lucas, Simon Egert, Bobby Harrold, Gillian Crossley, Mike Walker and the Morley friends.

My Lord Brachiano
Alas I make but repetition
Of what is ordinary and rialto talk,
And ballated, and would be play'd a' th' stage

John Webster
The White Devil

CONTENTS

THE DEN OF DELIGHTS

Mr. Mangan's morning had been ruined by the non-delivery of the Elvis. O'Connor's boy had promised it by lunchtime on his mother's life, so that it not arriving and Father Corrigan being twice down to see what had become of it had sent his blood pressure up and himself down to the local to berate youth in general and Frank O'Connor's boy in particular although normally he never took a glass before dusk.

'I was to have it by eleven, definite', he said. 'O'Connor's boy promised it on his mother's life.'

'His mother's dead,' Padraig Burke observed, pulling a half for himself.

'She is not.'

'She is so. Died this twelvemonth back, not a month after they moved down to Derry.'

'Then there's not the glimmer of a chance of my acquiring the goods and preserving my reputation.' Mr. Mangan's thin features contorted gloomily over his Guinness. 'What did she die of?'

'Blown up. The car was wired. It was meant for her all right because Frank was away in Dublin at the time and in any case his credentials are immaculate.'

'I can't believe it. She was a good republican, Maire.'

'She was. But only after she married Frank, so the story goes. She was born a Protestant. Her father was active in the marching season. No-one knew it hereabouts but when she went to Coleraine to bury him they say she was the one laid the sash across the coffin before they lowered it. Someone must have seen.'

'I had no idea, poor woman. A tragedy. And her son is going to be another when I get my hands on him.' Mr. Mangan put his glass down and began to fish in his pocket for change when a youth came into the bar. Short, and probably overweight, he was tightly packed into regulation biker gear of black boots, jeans and PVC jacket, zipped and studded. Clean-shaven, he had a pale, round face and close-cropped hair and several rings in the lobe of his left ear. He walked jauntily, a mobile phone pressed to his cheek.

He reached the bar, indicated his preference for a pint, then turned and leant back against the counter, talking into the handset in a self-important manner. 'I've just now come from Mangan's and it isn't there,' he said. 'No more is Mangan. Shop's shut.'

'And could that possibly be, young man, because Mangan has been waiting all the Christian hours for a person like yourself to show up?' Christy Mangan moved to face the young man, took the telephone from his hand and spoke into it:

'Is that you, Frank? What in heaven's name is going on? Where's my statue? I've been waiting all morning and Corrigan half a dozen times into the shop asking for it. I'll give you till three, Frank. If it's not here by then it's all over between you and me.' And between me and Corrigan, he thought, as he shut down the phone and placed it on the bar.

O'Connor's boy took the phone and tucked it inside his jacket. 'I don't know why you're so exercised at all,' he said peevishly. 'Mr. Mangan,' he added, as he felt the force of the older man's gaze. 'You know my da. He keeps his word. O'Connors keep their word.'

'Is that so? Well, correction, young man, but he's broken it already. I promised it to Father Corrigan early, since he didn't want too many people about to spoil the surprise of the evening. He was particular on the point.'

'I don't see why,' the boy said sulkily.

'It's not for you to see or not to see. It was supposed to be with me by lunchtime because Father Corrigan is a busy man who has set aside a particular portion of his particularly busy day to setting up the hall for the dance and to getting into position the Elvis which I promised him my faithful suppliers - that is the well-known haulage company of O'Connor senior and O'Connor junior - would supply. So you'll forgive me if I am not minded to be impressed by the performance of the O'Connor team so far.'

Mr. Mangan threw a glance in the direction of Padraig Burke and swung out of the pub, O'Connor's boy following at a distance.

Mr. Mangan's shop stood at the intersection of Collins and De Valera streets, enjoying two frontages and a sign, in gold lettering on a black background, which read *Mangan's Den Of* and, round the corner, *Delights*. A smaller notice in the window, hand written on yellowing card, informed: *All manner of articles sold and acquired*. Seventies dresses for a themed party? Mangan's was the place. Gangster outfits for your *Guys and Dolls* theatricals (with Bridie O'Dowd *delicious* as Miss Adelaide)? Mangan was your man. He rarely let you down, so that it remained an irony that the interior geography of his shop, an escarpment of gas cookers and chiffoniers, sewing machines and Carmen rollers, mirrors, lamps and oriental screens, never changed at all. Stacked precariously and at random, Mangan's delights hovered eternally, awaiting significance.

Mr. Mangan could see at once that between the time of his leaving the shop and his present return, a miracle had occurred. Larger than lifesize, with real sequins sparkling on the lapels of a bright white painted suit, and rays of sunlight glancing off ridges of fulgent black hair, his Elvis stood high on an open truck, legs apart, arms outstretched, red enamelled lips in pink, enamelled face open in silent song. He dominated the townscape like the Cristo Redentor of Rio, a quasi-mystical figure in the dull quiescence of early afternoon. Two copper-haired girls stood by the truck. Beside them, O'Connor's boy's motorcycle lay on the ground. His helmet rolled backwards and forwards in the gutter.

'Is he not something miraculous altogether?' Kathleen Mulligan leaned her forearms on the side of the truck, rested her chin on her hands and gazed up at the startlingly immobile face.

'Our ma remembers the day he died,' her sister said. 'She cried for a week, so she did. They heard it over the radio the day our da first came courting her. He had to leave off till she was over it. He said it was a terrible disincentive, the competition of a pop star and an icon.'

'Is it a saint he is now?'

'Of course not, stupid.'

'Only I just thought, with Father Corrigan ...'

'Don't be so witless, Kathleen. Anyway, Father Corrigan is only having the Elvis because Mr. Mangan couldn't get the Tina Turner. Father Corrigan said it wasn't important, it was size that mattered. I'm just saying that the way it was when Elvis died, he might as well have been a saint. Our ma would still rather go to Memphis than the Vatican if she won the lottery.'

'That's a terrible thing to say. It's sacrilegious.'

'Maybe it is and maybe it isn't. I'll tell you something, though. If Frank O'Connor's boy had not got it to Mr. Mangan by this very moment or sooner, Mr. Mangan was going to wring his neck and hang him out on the line to dry.' The girls giggled then fell silent as the boy and Mr. Mangan approached.

'Did I not persuade you the O'Connors could be relied upon?' Frank O'Connor's boy panted after Mr. Mangan.

'You were late.'

'Not so it mattered.'

'It always matters. Now we have to get it to Father Corrigan. Where's your driver gone?' Mr. Mangan saw that the driver's cab was empty.

'He went to see his auntie,' the elder girl volunteered. 'He said he should take the opportunity. He said he only gets to come out this way once in a -'

Mr. Mangan cut her short. 'Can you drive?'

The boy was re-establishing his bike against the kerb. 'Well I ... that is to say, I once ...'

'Get in,' Mr. Mangan ordered.

The boy climbed up into the driver's seat. He looked down miserably at the keys, swaying in the ignition, at the gears, at the inordinate distance he seemed now to be from the ground.

'Don't start her up yet. I want to check it's secure.' Mr. Mangan walked round the truck and saw that the figure was fastened to metal rings at the four corners of the truck by two ropes, each wound several times around its waist.

'It looks firm enough,' he said. 'Only they're very light, these effigies. They're made of nothing more than coated polystyrene and wire. So don't take it too fast, Michael Schumacher.' He patted the flank of the cab, like a trainer before a race.

'You can start her up now. The road's clear. But easy, mind. You know where the hall is, at the bottom of the hill.'

The boy pushed the gear stick into neutral and very gingerly turned the ignition. The engine rumbled into life.

'Do you or do you not want a ride with a star to paradise?' Mr. Mangan turned to the girls, nodding towards the truck.

They jumped up, heaving themselves over the side, and fell, laughing, to the floor. Kathleen wrapped herself around the hard flared trouser bottoms and painted patent shoes. *'Love me tender, love me true ...'* she sang wildly to the small group of people who had gathered at the scene and now fell in behind Mr. Mangan, forming a little procession which advanced slowly, almost reverently, down the narrow street.

'Stay in two!' Mr. Mangan shouted to the boy, as the engine lurched suddenly from one gear to another.

The boy, sweating, sighed with relief. His left foot hovered over the clutch, his right foot came off the accelerator. With one hand on the wheel, and the other ready on the handbrake, he prayed for a sudden miracle of timing and co-ordination when the moment to stop would arrive.

He saw the hall a moment before Mr. Mangan shouted to him again. A low stone building, with porch and weathered lintel, it stood opposite the garage. Over the lintel, facing the one pump, the words *The Ballroom of Romance* had been newly painted in white. Along the walls, slogans and graffiti had faded to various stages of illegibility. The legend *Free Bobby Sands* could just be distinguished. Father Corrigan stood in the road.

The boy took a deep breath, jammed his foot down on the clutch and pulled the handbrake. The vehicle juddered violently and stalled. The girls screamed and the Elvis wobbled, but did not fall.

'You young fool. Are you not acquainted with the gears at all?' Mr. Mangan raged at the boy, as his effigy swayed before his eyes.

The boy was past caring. He tumbled down and sat on the grass verge. Father Corrigan was beaming. 'Is it not a beautiful representation?' he declared expansively. 'You've done us proud, Christy Mangan, so you have.' Tall, florid, Father Corrigan was a vigorous man in his early forties who had brought a breath of fresh air into the small community when he arrived from the south two years ago. It was he who had put Mr. Mangan on to the small Londonderry business which made the polystyrene models that had proved such an attraction at the dances and discos in the Inishowen peninsula, especially in the summer, when the visitors came.

'They'll always hire them out to the likes of you, Christy. But they're beginning to sell them now - Isle of Man, Skegness, all over. They're hoping for America soon. It's a growing concern, no doubt about it.'

The girls toppled down from the trailer. Mr. Mangan climbed in and went to undo the ropes.

'No, no. Christy Mangan. Don't be troubling yourself. I have my own men here.' He indicated two men whom Mr. Mangan had taken for bouncers standing in the doorway to the ballroom of romance. At a sign from Father Corrigan they came forward and swung themselves up on to the truck. Mr. Mangan took Father Corrigan's hand and jumped rather awkwardly to the ground. He stood beside the truck, taking in the operation.

The men moved around the truck undoing the ropes. As the last one was loosened the bigger man moved to the centre and put his arm around the Elvis waist. He braced himself, and Mr. Mangan saw that he staggered slightly as the painted body fell against him. His partner was beside him instantly and together they tipped the figure on to its side and laid it very carefully on the floor of the truck. They straightened, then one of them jumped from the truck and unfastened the back, releasing a metal ramp. He pulled it to the ground, checked it for fastness and mounted it. The men bent down and put their arms under the body. 'On three!' The first jerk took it up to their waists, the second to their shoulders. Slowly and carefully they manoeuvred the figure down the ramp to the ground, stooping slightly as they went.

'Nice and easy, boys,' Father Corrigan said loudly, moving in beside them, 'nice and easy.' And in a lower tone, close to their faces, 'I said, *easy.*'

The crowd moved forward, holding out their hands to touch and admire, but Father Corrigan was on to his men. 'Take him in the hall, boys, and set him up. I'll be with you directly.' He held out a protective arm between his prize and his flock, and signalled the crowd back.

'Tonight, my friends. Wait until tonight. You'll not be disappointed, I assure you. We'll light him up and you shall see him in all his splendour.'

They watched as the prone likeness of the singer was carried into the hall. Father Corrigan's men walked slowly, Father Corrigan beside them, a protective hand on the painted white suit.

'Is there not something sinister about the sight of him, shiny and stiff like that? When his whole life was spent gyrating his hips and pumping his guitar.' The elder Mulligan girl watched the body quizically, her head to one side. 'Where is his guitar anyways?'

'The guitar!' Father Corrigan turned abruptly and made towards the truck. But Kathleen was there before him and had run up the ramp. She picked the instrument up from the floor and handed it to her sister, who had cut back with her. Then she jumped down and the two girls ran into the hall where the men were erecting the figure on the stage. They threw the strap over its head and placed the guitar carefully between the huge, pink, inert hands.

'That's better. Almost lifelike now, isn't he? Not exactly sexy, I shouldn't say, but lifelike anyways. When he's all lit up, and in the dark, you might imagine yourself believing that he was going to play. He was heavy though, wasn't he?' She looked up at his minders. 'I'll swear to God he was, the way you were carrying him.' She watched their faces. 'There's something inside him, isn't there?'

'Shush, Kathleen,' her sister said, 'what are you saying?'

'I'm saying there's something inside him. I'll swear to God there is.' She pressed her cheek against the inanimate idol and made a fist to tap it with the back of her knuckles, but Father Corrigan was behind her and caught her wrist lightly in his hand.

'He was light as a feather, Kathleen,' he said easily. 'Isn't that the truth of it, boys?'

'Light as a feather, Father,' they said, 'light as a feather.'

THE HEADMASTER'S CHOICE

'Sir.'

'Yes, Parker?'

'Sir. May I make an appointment to see you?'

'Yes. What about?'

'It's a sensitive matter, Sir. I'd prefer to discuss it in private.'

'When do you want to come?'

'Any time, Sir. This evening, if that would suit you, after supper. Around nine, perhaps?'

'Yes. Come to my room at nine.'

'Thank you, Sir.'

Mr. Raleigh had not wanted a House.

'I am a bachelor,' he had protested, at interview. 'I have no domestic experience of boys. I'm not sure that I would be suitable.'

'Are you homosexual?'

'No, I am not.'

'Then I don't see a problem. I have on offer the post of Senior Classics master and, since Singleton's death at Easter, a House. It carries extra salary and free accommodation. Consider it carefully before you turn it down.'

'I had not thought to have to consider it.'

'I had not thought Singleton was going to get himself killed on a school trip in Shropshire.'

'Perhaps I could go away and think about it.'

'Please do. But think about it positively. This is a happy school and I feel you would fit in very well.'

After eight years' teaching in two Catholic institutions, Geoffrey Raleigh felt ready to head a department. He would probably not receive a better offer than this. He decided to accept the somewhat dubious gift of Edmund Campion House.

In his first term, the headmaster expelled two boys. Neither was from Campion, but the head called a meeting of all Housemasters and urged vigilance.

'Cigarettes I am inclined to turn a blind eye to. But drugs, no. We can't afford it. Watch for unusual activity, and activities involving unlikely groups of boys. Look out for loners. Use your senior boys, your House Captains and Prefects. Never forget that this is an unnatural environment and in unnatural environments you get unnatural practices. Mr. Raleigh, a moment before you go.'

As the others filed out he drew Raleigh aside.

'How are things going? Getting to know your boys?'

'I think so, slowly. I was glad they weren't mine who were expelled.'

'So am I. It would have been a rotten start. I had to fire one of Singleton's a couple of years back. It nearly finished him. Mind you, the old chap was going a bit soggy in later years. I was dreading having to ask him to step aside. The House was his life.'

'What exactly happened to him?'

'We don't know. They were walking Offa's Dyke. He had taken half a dozen boys. It was the kind of thing he liked to do. Three of them, who had binoculars, had followed Singleton up a slope in search of ravens. Singleton thought he had heard a call. It was scree, and slippery, and he must have lost his footing because according to Parker he simply slid away. He fell about three hundred feet. Parker found him dead and took charge of the group. Parker is very sound. He was my choice. I felt you should have some sort of power structure in place when you arrived. I think you will find him a help.'

Mr. Raleigh did not like Parker. He was his Head of House and a Prefect, but he did not like him. He was a tall, loose-limbed, plausible boy with blonde hair worn a little too long, sweaters a little too baggy, trousers a little too low. He scrubbed up well for Open Days in suit, silver and grey-striped Prefects' tie and hair slicked back with gel, and parents other than Mr. and Mrs. Parker admired him as he dazzled round the Great Hall, but all the same Mr. Raleigh did not like him and did not trust him. He felt himself to be one move behind Parker, without knowing what the move was, or when it might have taken place.

And now it was nine-fifteen and Parker had not arrived and Mr. Raleigh was annoyed. He disliked a casual attitude to time. Perhaps he had not been specific enough. He replayed the conversation in his head.

'Ah, Parker. There you are. I thought we said nine.'

'Indeed we did, Sir. And I apologise.' Parker sank into an armchair and draped his arms languidly over the sides. 'I came across a couple of fourth-formers having a bit of a ruck in the quad and I thought I should sort it out before things turned nasty.'

'I see. Who were they?'

'Oh, they weren't Campion, Sir.'

'Ah. Well done. I think.' He withheld the 'thankyou' he sensed was expected.

'I think so too, Sir. Always best to nip trouble in the bud, isn't it. Which is why I have come to see you.'

'Yes?'

'It's a rather delicate matter, Sir, and as yet I have no proof, but I felt you should be alerted. It's Rhys-Evans, Sir.'

'Yes?'

'He's a bit of a weirdo, wouldn't you agree?'

'We can accommodate weirdos, Parker.'

'Oh, indeed, Sir. But I'm wondering if his behaviour isn't beginning to verge on the suspicious. He spends hours and hours in the computer room, yet if I stop by and ask him what he's doing, he shuts it down. Instantly. I just think he might be up to something.'

'What, exactly?'

'I don't know, Sir. Downloading porn, perhaps. Selling pictures to the younger boys. That kind of thing, Sir.'

'What makes you think that? Are there any such pictures around? Or evidence that he fraternizes with younger boys?'

'Not to my knowledge, Sir. But I think we should keep an eye. I was wondering if we might have a private word with him here in your study. I might be able to get more out of him than you would, Sir.'

'I think not, Parker. I appreciate your vigilance, but I see no immediate cause for concern.'

'But Sir -'

'You have alerted me, Parker. And I am grateful. You can leave it with me.'

'Are you going to get him in, Sir?'

'I'll think about it. Thank you again, Parker.' Mr. Raleigh had risen and the boy was forced to follow suit. 'I am grateful for your concern.'

Left alone, Mr. Raleigh returned to his desk and considered. Rhys-Evans, a small, pale, bespectacled boy in the Lower Fifth, was little known to him. He went to his files and pulled out copies of previous Reports. They were not illuminating. Rhys-Evans was a 'B' stream boy, well-behaved, punctual, quiet, helpful, underweight and myopic. He had no discernible particular aptitudes and did not shine on the sports field. He had not taken part in the House play, *Widowers' Houses*, but had helped with props and scenery. Average. A very average boy. Unremarkable in any way except that he had somehow incurred Parker's dislike. Mr. Raleigh wondered how, apart from shutting down his computer every time Parker came in. Perhaps that was enough. Control freaks see subversion where often there is none. Mr. Raleigh felt that on the whole Rhys-Evans was entitled to his privacy.

'Did you see R-E, Sir?' Parker caught him a few days later as he was crossing the quad.

'I'm sorry?'

'R-E, Sir.' Mr. Raleigh baulked at the collusion the abbreviation implied. 'You said you were going to see him.'

'No, Parker. You will recall that I said you could leave the matter in my hands. And I would prefer it if such things were not discussed in the quad.'

'Of course, Sir. Then may I see you after Evening Prayers?'

Mr. Raleigh sighed. 'If you wish. I will be in my study.'

'Sir.' Parker walked smartly into the room after a peremptory knock. 'I don't think you are taking the Rhys-Evans business seriously enough. I'm quite sure he's up to something. I caught him fiddling about under his bed.'

'What do you mean, 'caught'? I don't believe I authorised you to spy on anyone, Parker.'

'No, Sir. But when I was checking the study-dorms last night he seemed to be hiding something under his bed. When I asked him what he was up to, he said Nothing.'

'That's pretty much par for the course, I would have thought. We must remember that every boy has a right to a certain amount of privacy, Parker. Otherwise life becomes intolerable.'

'I realise that, Sir. But I still think Rhys-Evans has got something going on. I believe we should investigate.'

'We?'

'You, Sir, of course. You might wish me to accompany you.'

'Thank you, Parker, but I will deal with it myself.'

'Soon, Sir? I think the headmaster likes us to act on these things pretty swiftly.'

Raleigh absorbed the veiled threat. 'In my own time. Now, if there's nothing else, I have a lot of paper work to get through.'

Mr. Raleigh called Rhys-Evans to his room the following evening.

'Rhys-Evans. Come in and sit down. Push those books off the sofa and make yourself a space. How are things going for you this term? Work all right? Any problems?'

'I don't think so, Sir.'

'Good. I'm glad. You know that if you ever need to talk, I am always available.'

Rhys-Evans looked surprised. 'Thank you, Sir.'

'And friends? You have plenty of friends?'

'Yes, Sir.'

'You're not particularly keen on sport, I know. I was wondering how you spend your free time?'

'On the computer, Sir.'

'Yes, I'd heard. Don't you feel you spend a bit too much of your time in front of a screen?'

'I don't know, Sir. Perhaps.'

'Just a thought. I'd like to see you taking a more active part in the life of the House. Music, perhaps, or a Club. You understand what I'm saying. All work and no play....'

'Yes, Sir.' Rhys-Evans screwed up his face in thought. 'I belong to the Science Club, Sir. But I don't play an instrument.' He paused. 'Did you want me to take up an instrument, Sir?'

Mr. Raleigh smiled. 'No, no. I'm not trying to steer you in any direction. I simply want you to be aware of what's on offer here, and take advantage. So you're not spending quite so much time on your own.'

'I see, Sir. Thank you, Sir.'

'Good. Now. What's your dorm like?'

'It's all right, Sir. A bit of a mess at the moment.'

'Mind if we walk up and take a look? I'd like to see how you're set up.'

'No, Sir.'

They walked up the worn stone staircase, Rhys-Evans leading, to the study-dorm he shared with Hedges, a rugby jock who was hoping for a West of England trial and spent his free time playing sport or training. Rhys-Evans's side was tidy, the bed made, a counterpane pulled over, touching the floor.

'Good hiding place,' Mr. Raleigh said.

'No, Sir.' Rhys-Evans stood in front of the bed, legs apart, hands behind his back, pale eyes staring past Mr. Raleigh through small, round spectacles.

'Then you won't mind if I look.'

'No, Sir.'

Mr. Raleigh stooped to lift up the counterpane.

'No, Sir. I mean, *No, Sir. Don't!*'

Mr. Raleigh stopped, arrested by the urgency in the boy's voice. 'What is it, Rhys-Evans?'

For several seconds boy and master stood facing each other, their eyes locked. Then, without shifting his gaze, the boy said slowly and clearly,

'A bomb.'

'*What?*'

'A bomb, Sir.'

'How do you mean, a bomb?'

'That's what's under the bed, Sir. That's why you mustn't touch anything under there. Nothing must be moved.'

'Is it ... live?'

'Oh yes, Sir. It detonates on impact.'

'God. How did it get there?'

'I made it, Sir.'

'What do you mean, you made it?'

'From the Internet, Sir. I followed instructions.'

'Whatever for?'

'I found them, Sir, when I was surfing. I wanted to see if it could be done.'

'How long has it been there?'

'A week. I am trying to find out how to dismantle it, Sir. The Internet gives no instructions, but I'm sure they must exist, in a library book or something. The Colditz prisoners made a glider from diagrams in a library book.'

'Over a period of time, Rhys-Evans. Which is something we don't have. You realise how serious this is? You realise the whole school could blow up at any minute?'

'Not really, Sir. I've positioned it so it can't be moved. Provided nobody touches anything, it's quite safe.'

'The room will be sealed off and you and Hedges will sleep in the San. I shall call in the Army and a bomb disposal unit. And in the meantime, you will explain yourself to the headmaster.'

'The difficulty, Geoffrey,' the headmaster said, 'will be in keeping it out of the press. How many people know about it?'

'As far as I'm aware, only Rhys-Evans and ourselves.'

'Hedges?'

'Rhys-Evans says not, and I believe him. Hedges is not very observant and his side of the dorm is a complete pickle. He spends all his time playing sport and training.'

'Then we may get away with it. What reason did you give for sealing off the room?'

'Rats.'

'All right. And when do they send in the bomb disposal squad?'

'They're on their way.'

'Good. Make sure they use the back drive and rear entrance. They'll want the House evacuated, I feel sure. Try to keep it as low-key as you can. I don't want a spectacle.'

'Of course not. They know that.'

'What a nightmare. Rhys-Evans will have to go, of course. I've told him.'

'Go?'

'Expelled. He understands.'

'Expelled?'

'Of course. What did you expect?'

'Isn't that a bit severe?'

'For trying to blow up the school? I don't think so.'

'He didn't have that intention, headmaster. He just ... wanted to see if it could be done.'

'I am far too angry to argue the point at present. And frankly, Geoffrey, I'm surprised at you. How could this have gone on without your knowledge? Didn't anyone have an inkling that Rhys-Evans was up to something?'

Mr. Raleigh wrestled briefly with his conscience. 'No', he said.

Parker was loitering at the top of the drive, hands in pockets (a privilege of Prefects) when Mr. and Mrs. Rhys-Evans's Volvo arrived to collect their son. Mr. Rhys-Evans's face betrayed no emotion, Mrs. Rhys-Evans had been crying. Their son's trunk, boxes, sports gear and personal computer were packed swiftly into the boot. Mr. Raleigh came out and spoke briefly to the parents.

'I'm so sorry. I tried very hard to dissuade the headmaster, but he felt he had no choice. Explosives, you understand. Your son is not a bad boy, just misguided - and a little too inventive. I hope you will find another school for him. Please come to me if you need help, or a reference. I wish him the best of luck.'

They shook hands, and Rhys-Evans emerged from the House and crossed in front of Parker towards the car.

'*Filthy pervert,*' Parker snarled.

Rhys-Evans paused, startled.

'I know it wasn't rats. I saw them come to do your study over last night. Serve you right if you don't get banged up. What did they find? What did they find, eh, in your stinking little pit? *Porn pedlar.*'

Rhys-Evans looked at him blankly then climbed wearily into the car and slammed the door.

THE FITTING

'You should come earlier in the year. Or later. Venice is full of people like you in the summer. Visitors. People who don't belong here.'

'The date was chosen for me.'

'Of course. I simply point it out to you, *cara*. Venice in August is not Venice at her best. But for a party, a celebration, people find it convenient.'

We walk together along the narrow pavement, la Signora Fazio, Rodolfo's exquisite mother, and myself. It is early morning, the mist has not yet lifted from the canals, the sun not yet drawn the rank summer smells into the air. Barges are on the water, delivering fresh linen to the hotels. A few *gondolieri* are out, their oars breaking the water softly, regularly. If this is a bad month to be in Venice, at least it is a good time. *'Buon giorno Signora, Signorina! Buon giorno!'* Traders are opening up their shops, clattering down the sun blinds. Smells of freshly made coffee and pastries leak out into the street.

'Merda!' My future mother-in-law's expensively shod foot has encountered something unpleasant. She leans against me, her burgundy fingernails gripping my shoulder. Lifting her foot, she turns the sole inwards to inspect the outrage. 'Filthy dogs!' she says. 'Get a tissue from my bag, Jennifer, *cara*. Wipe it. Quickly. We have not so much time.'

Struggling with the clasp, I find a packet of tissues and, still taking her weight, extract one and bend to wipe the sole of her elegant cream sandal. Her ankle is thin, a slim gold bracelet against the pale skin. I hold it with my left hand and make a half-hearted attack on the faeces.

'Is no good. You are spreading it only. *'Santo cielo!'*

She releases her hold on me and brings her foot down on the pavement, pressing and turning the sole into the stones, instep high, like a dancer.

'I can buy new', she says. 'Come. *Andiamo*. Valli is *un maestro*. You will be pleased with him, I think.'

Around the corner, in the *Calle Madonetta*, Signor Valli waits at the entrance to his premises. I say 'premises' for I can see at once that Signor Valli is a man of some dignity but also honesty. 'Shop' would not be an appropriate description of the network of intercommunicating rooms, on several floors, which lie behind him, but then neither would 'couture house'. There is Armani in Venice, there is Valentino, but Signor Valli is the little secret of women in the know, and he will clothe many of those who will attend the engagement party, the *festa di fidanzamento* which la Signora is giving for Rodolfo and myself this weekend. I am to be presented to Rodolfo's many relatives and will meet for the first time his elder brother Massimo and his new wife Isabella Giorgione. Isabella's family is believed to be descended from the fifteenth century Venetian painter. They were married last summer at *Santa Maria della Salute*. According to Rodolfo's mother, it was the union of two great houses.

Signor Valli has risen early to accommodate us, but no detail has been overlooked in the preparation of his *toilette*. He is small, lean, with thick greying hair well cut and styled away from the face. His dark eyes are deep set but lively, only a slight yellowing of the whites betraying his age. He wears a light tan and a cream linen suit, hand stitched, and blue silk shirt, the top buttons fashionably undone. A tape measure hangs round his neck. As Italians go, he is understated. He wears no jewellery, apart from a thin gold Patek Philippe on his left wrist, at which he glances as we arrive.

'*Signora! Signorina! Benvenuti!* My day is now a happy one!' He holds out his arms in welcome and la Signora responds, bending slightly to take his two kisses, ruffling the back of his hair lightly as she leaves his embrace.

'*Allora, Eduardo! Come va?*'

'*Sono molto felice di rivederLa, Signora!* Better for seeing you again.'

He smoothes his hair and turns to guide us through a room in which several women are sitting, under artificial lights, at sewing machines, heads bent in concentration, hands turning swathes of rich fabric this way and that, fast female fingers at tiny chicanes. In a small back room, which has a flight of stairs, rails of almost completed clothes, and a curtained area for changing, a young girl, kneeling, works on the hem of a pale oyster silk suit. Her model, a dressmaker's dummy, carries it quite as well as I shall do.

'Silvana', he says. *'Ecco la Signora Fazio e la Signorina Brown.'*

Silvana rises and drops an awkward greeting, her hands held out in explanation. A velvet bracelet of pins encircles her left wrist, pins cover the lapels of her light jacket, neatly arranged, Air Force style; she has one between the thumb and forefinger of her right hand, and her lips grip several more.

'Ah. She is my *tesoro*, my little pin girl. Like your little match girl, no?' He puts his arm around my shoulders and steers me towards the makeshift changing room. 'I will bring your suit, *Signorina*. And then we shall see. *Vediamo davvero.* '

In the cubicle behind the curtain I slip off my skirt and blouse. My new underwear no longer seems sophisticated. I am glad Rodolfo's mother has not accompanied me. I feel sure she would have detected the chain store labels.

'Permesso?' An arm is thrust round the curtain and my suit handed in. From my brief sketch, something ravishing has been produced: a narrow skirt, taffeta lined, and short fitted jacket with wide neck and long sleeves, exquisitely cut. I put it on with extreme caution. The pins in the lining of the skirt assault my stockings. I have little scratches down my arms from the tight sleeves. I pull back the curtain and step into the room.

'Splendido!' la Signora exclaims. *'Meraviglioso!* Eduardo, I congratulate you.' She hugs, then quickly releases him, dropping on one knee to swivel the skirt a little. She holds the seams in with her hands, stretching the silk across my hips.

'A little taking in ... here ... and here. Don't you think so? She can take it a little tighter, yes?'

'Certo, Signora. Certo. But you like it, yes? *Le piace?'*

'Mi piace molto.'

'E bella, la Signorina.'

'Si. E bella. She has no style, of course. *Allora*, perhaps with time ...'

Signor Valli removes a few pins from each seam and repositions them adroitly. He takes my hips and turns me slowly round in front of the mirror. '*Va bene. Ora va bene. Signora! Signora Fazio! Viene e vedere.*'

La Signora has wandered through the workroom and out into the street. At his call she returns, a cigarette between her fingers, a slim gold lighter still cupped in the palm of her hand.

'*A no, Signora. Per favore. Non e permesso.* Think of the danger, the fabrics, the *stoffa*.'

'You are not in danger, Eduardo. *Mio Dio!* I smoke in my bedroom. Do I set myself on fire? I don't think so.'

'*Per favore, Signora. Per cortesia.* I cannot afford... my fabrics are very ... you know yourself ...'

'Who is paying? Eh? Who is paying? I am paying. You want that I pay more?'

'I think you do not understand, *Signora*. My new agreement, my new insurance, it does not cover ...'

'Agreement! Insurance!' What a small man you are turning into, Eduardo. I had begun to think of you as an artist, a *couturier*.'

They stand facing each other, la Signora holding his gaze.

Suddenly he reaches forward and grips her wrist, forcing the lighter to fall from her hand. The cigarette wobbles between her fingers.

'Take it outside. You ... make...my ...clothes ....stale.'

For a second she hesitates, then picks up the lighter and saunters out through the open door and into the street. Slowly and exaggeratedly, with a wide sweep of her arm, she tosses the cigarette into the water.

Signor Valli has given Silvana some muttered instructions and left by the back staircase. I feel his light tread above us.

'Where is he?'

'He has gone to his rooms, Signora.'

Without a word she brushes past us and follows him up.

'You have known your mother-in-law long?' Silvana is managing a conversation between pursed lips. She speaks no English.

'She isn't my mother-in-law. Not yet.' Under Rodolfo's tutelage my Italian is now almost fluent, a fact which his mother has not quite understood.

'She is a very beautiful woman.' She raises her pretty face. '*Molto elegante.*'

'Oh yes.'

'She was a Foscari before her marriage. And a model. With one of the great houses, Balenciaga I think. Signor Valli admires her very much. He says she shows his clothes to great advantage, her height, her red hair, her skin.' Silvana works around me, unpinning and pinning seams, adjusting shoulders, loosening armholes. She works deftly but with a purpose, so that occasionally I flinch from the scrape of pins against my skin.

'*Scusi, Signorina.*'

In the next room the machinists whirr and pause. In the brief intervals of silence I hear voices upstairs, the clink of glasses, movement, and ...? I strain to hear, but the machines start up practically as soon as they leave off, an almost continuous symphony of beehive music.

Silvana is working on the hem now, pushing it against my knees with the back of her hand, letting it fall, rising and stepping back a few paces to inspect, to re-pin, to step back again, and again, and again.

'I think it's fine now.'

'It must be *perfetto*', she says. '*Per la Signora, perfetto.*'

'But it's for me. I am not so fussy.'

She smiles. She tells me that la Signora comes to Signor Valli every year, for summer clothes. La Signora thinks that Signor Valli has a way with linens, and silk linen weaves. He makes her skirts and jackets and trouser suits - some of them she wears even in *Milano*, Silvana believes.

'You have met her husband, the doctor?'

'Once, in London. He seemed very charming. He arrives this evening from Milan.'

'He is a great doctor here in Italy. A great doctor for women. He gives treatments for women. Women who cannot have babies, they come from all over Italy to see him. One woman, she was forty-two. Forty-two and no babies. She came from Palermo to see Doctor Fazio and he made her five babies. Five. All at once. It was a miracle, no? But I think he made too many.'

'Definitely too many.'

'La Signora says that when I am married, if I have no babies, Doctor Fazio will help me. He will not charge. He is a wonderful man. He makes women happy. You will be married in Venice, *Signorina*?'

'I don't think so.' I explain that Rodolfo does not feel quite so Italian as his brother Massimo. That, working in London on the English desk of his Milanese bank, his colleagues call him Rod and many are unaware that he is Italian, so good is his English, so European has the City become.

'La Signora will be *desolata*. She loves to arrange. She is *un po romantica*, I think.'

Silvana has finished and rises from her knees as Signor Valli comes down into the room, lightly, with the step of a much younger man. He takes me by the hips once more and turns me slowly round, frowning, his gaze taking in every line, every seam, every nuance and shadow of the silk. He makes the tiniest adjustment under the bust, on the shoulders, at the wrists. Eventually he is satisfied.

'*E perfetto*,' he says, standing away.

'You will send it to the *palazzo*?' La Signora has joined us, and watches me walk back to the changing cubicle.

'*Naturalmente*.'

'By Friday. We must have it by Friday. The *Festa* is on Saturday, but I must have everything at the house by Friday'.

'*D'accordo*. I am your slave, Signora.'

'I know it.'

Stepping out of the changing room, I see her take his face roughly in her hands and press it to her. He captures her hand, pressing it swiftly and urgently to his lips.

'*Beatrice ...*'

'*Allora. Ci partiamo*'. La Signora has seen me. She propels us quickly to the door. Signor Valli follows. Out on the pavement, he has recovered the height he seemed momentarily to have lost.

'It has been a pleasure, *Signorina*, a pleasure. You will come again? And might I be allowed to hope, perhaps, that for your wedding dress you may consider the house of Valli...'

I make a gesture which may be interpreted as anything from acquiescence to regretful refusal. 'You are very kind, *Signor. Mille grazie.*'

'Your wedding dress! *Beh!*' She turns me away. 'Valli, he is nothing. He is a provincial, a peasant. Your wedding dress indeed. For your wedding dress we go to *Milano.*'

Taking my arm, she steps briskly down the street and turns the corner, neatly avoiding the little pile of excrement that had trapped her earlier.

INCIDENT ON PLATFORM FIFTEEN

Mervyn is already exhausted by the holiday. Three weeks in continental Europe have played havoc with his digestion and self-esteem and he stands now on Platform I5 waiting, with weary anticipation, for the 10.38 to East Grinstead to arrive. The hot August morning promises a day of relentless sun. He looks at the sunlight glancing off the rails below him, off the coke cans and addicts' foils and other random detritus caught between the platforms, between the great urban movements of commuting life. England was filthy, disgusting. He can't think how he had been persuaded to come away.

He moves along the platform and sinks slowly on to a wood and concrete bench, pushing aside a supermarket bag and open sandwich bubble, the remains of a tuna mayonnaise curling in the heat. At the kiosk, further down the platform, his wife is buying drinks and a morning paper.

'You want a paper, honey?' she calls over, briefly interrupting her transaction.

He shakes his head. Yes, he would like a paper. He would like the Cincinnati Enquirer and he would like to be in Cincinnati reading it. This world of Becks and Posh and Blair and Merkel and Euro and non-Euro, he neither wants to know about nor read about. It is not his world, and thank God for it. It is not Alison's world either, though she rails endlessly against losing the pound and British sovereignty. She left England years ago, to marry him. They have children, a daughter and a son, and five grandchildren who, most years, spend at least part of the summer with them at their cabin on Lake Erie. They are an American family, an all-American family. All except Alison. She has never taken U.S. citizenship, and it still rankles.

Alison has organised the holiday - their European Grand Tour, she calls it. A week in Rome, a week in Athens, a week in Paris, and now this last lap, eight days in London with rail trips around the country - Canterbury, Durham, Oxford, Windsor. Today it is Horsham, change at East Grinstead, because Alison's ancestors are buried there, in the graveyard of St. Andrew's Church, and so a pilgrimage has been incorporated into this month of almost unremitting culture. Mervyn is in charge of the tickets, that is to say he has them in his breast pocket. He puts his hand inside his jacket and checks. Alison has bought them, she has popped down to Victoria Station early this morning from their hotel in Pimlico. Two Senior Citizens' Rail Rovers, valid for seven days. Anywhere in the British Isles. Any network. It might seem a lot of money to shell out all at once, but really it's terrific value. Why don't they do this kind of deal back home? Alison's enthusiasm generally leaves him enervated. He has been put in charge of the tickets, he apprehends, to somehow secure his involvement in today's expedition.

The planning of the holiday has kept Alison happy for nearly a year, the floor of their ranch-style condominium spread with maps, tourist guides and timetables, Alison on hands and knees calculating connections, exploring opportunities.

'You want to see Canterbury, honey?'

'Sure, if you do.'

'Oh, Mervyn. Try to show a little interest,' looking up good-humouredly, pushing a strand of grey, curly hair from her face.

'It's your trip. You plan it. I've said I'm happy to go.'

'You know you're not. Not really. But it may be our last chance to go together. Who knows. And I've never really been back, you know. Only for mother's funeral.'

'That's it, then. We go.'

And so he has seen the Mona Lisa, he has gazed on the face of Agamemnon, he has thrown coins in the Fountain of Trevi. Not that these things have done him any particular good, but they have made Alison happy. And he will never have to do any of them again.

On reflection, he thinks, as a non-stop train rumbles past, Paris was the worst. The hotel, a little find of Alison's in the Marais, was not what he would have called a hotel at all, more a collection of bed-sits in a tall, crumbling building, a terrifying concierge sitting on the landing between the lift and their room. What was she doing there, morning and night? Did she never go home? Alison told him that he must tip her when they left, he had no idea what for. She had made their stay worse, not better, an intimidating presence to be negotiated each time he went to his room. So he did that. He said, 'Au revoir', which was about the extent of his competence in the language, and handed her a Euro. She held it out between her thumb and forefinger in apparent disbelief and he assumed that she swore, which tipped him over the edge. Fumbling in his pocket for a handful of small denomination U.S. coins he pulled them out and flung them into her lap. She spat, and he slipped quickly into the lift and pressed the button. He knew that his blood pressure had shot up.

Alison was waiting for him in the vestibule, having settled the bill.

'That go all right?'

'Oh fine,' he said.

Alison has left the kiosk and found a nice English couple to talk to. He knows that they will be a nice English couple, they always are. Without hearing it, he can track the conversation. Yes, they are going down to Horsham to trace her ancestors. Most of them are buried in the churchyard there. Such a lovely day for it, so lucky. She has telephoned the vicar in advance so that she may see the Parish Register. Her husband, he's over there on the seat -'All right, honey?' - doesn't quite share her enthusiasm for family trees, but she intends to start one when she gets back home. Families need to have a sense of their history, don't you agree? The nice couple agree. How long has she been in the States? Oh, more than forty years now. She used to be a Ward Sister at The Westminster - you remember, before it merged with Chelsea, and moved to the Fulham Road? - before going to Canada to take up a post in Vancouver. Except that she never got to Vancouver. She met Mervyn travelling across America on a Greyhound bus and... 'he swept me off my feet' drifts over to him. He wonders how true this is or was, though he generally accedes to it. It has become part of the folklore.

*

A train pulls in - 'Not this one, honey'- Alison calls out, though she knows he knows this - and the nice couple board it. They are replaced on the platform by an elegant oriental woman, taller than is customary, cool on this hot day. She is carefully and expensively dressed, a straight-skirted linen frock, leather-belted, high-heeled shoes and designer handbag. A long umbrella is an unnecessary accessory, its distinctive Burberry checks neatly furled. Alison smiles as she passes to join her husband on the seat. The Japanese woman smiles politely back and bows.

'Beautiful manners, haven't they, the Japanese.' Alison has settled herself and pulled out the schedule. 'They could certainly teach Americans a thing or two.' Oh yes. Just as they taught us in the early hours of a Sunday morning in December 1941. Three thousand American casualties, two thousand fatalities. One thousand, one hundred and two sailors dead. Which number had been his father, of the U.S. Naval Pacific Command, aboard the Arizona, just twenty-three years old? And less than a hundred Japanese lives lost. Oh yes, they could teach Americans a thing or two. *Wai Momi*, the Hawaiians call the place. Pearl Waters. They also call it *Puuloa*, home of the queen of the sharks, protectress of humans. Which humans.

'Honey, could you check the tickets?'
   'I just did.'
   'Where are they?'
   'They're here, in my breast pocket'. He draws them out to show to her and at that moment a non-stop express train, hurtling through the station before them, makes him jump, or causes a sudden draught of air, he doesn't know which. Whatever it may be, the tickets have left his hand and are now lying, fluttering feebly, between the rails in front of them.

'*Mervyn!*' Alison screams, rushing to the edge. 'What have you *done?*"
   'I don't know what happened. I...'

'You are so *stupid.* I should never have let you have them. I should have looked after them myself. That's four hundred pounds down the tube.'

'We could try getting the Station Manager...'

'Oh don't talk such garbage. There are no such things as Station Managers any more. What century are you living in? You and the Fat Controller. Nobody will give us our money back. Nobody will replace them. Nobody gives a damn.' She has slumped back on to the bench and is wailing angrily. 'It's only my whole holiday ruined, that's all.'

The Japanese woman has approached, unheard against Alison's sobs. Unable to address herself to Alison, she bows to Mervyn.

'Excuse, please.'

'Yeah. What is it? What do you want?'

'Gum, please?'

'What?'

'Yes please, chewing gum.'

'Chrissake. You kill our sailors, you bomb our airmen...'

'Shut up, Mervyn.' Alison has roused herself and is rooting in her handbag. She locates a packet of Wrigleys and hands it to the woman who unwraps a strip and without moving away places it in her mouth and begins to work the gum, very deliberately, as if giving a demonstration in the ancient art of gum-chewing. It looks like hard work. It looks as if it might be harming her tiny jaw. Finally, covering her mouth with one hand, with the other she extracts the ball of gum and delicately, with her painted fingers, places it carefully on the tip of her furled umbrella.

Walking to the edge of the platform she leans forward and stabs one of the tickets with the point of the umbrella. Adhering easily to the gum it is raised up and handed ceremoniously to Alison. The second ticket is similarly retrieved and presented. Then the woman removes the gum from the tip of her umbrella with the foil in which it was wrapped, screws it up, folds it inside a tissue and, after a quick look around the station for a refuse bin, places it in her bag.

'Oh, thank you. Thank you so much,' Alison is trying to grasp the woman's hand, but she is backing away, nodding and smiling.

'That was just brilliant. How did you ...?'

'I see it in a movie in Tokyo one time. Very nice movie. American. In Japan, American very nice, very good.'

She smiles, bows and excuses herself, returning to take up her position on the platform, waiting.

'Wasn't that something?' Alison turns, beaming, to her husband. 'Whoever would have thought it. Beautiful people aren't they, the Japanese. Beautiful manners.'

THE DARRAS

Sometimes, on an outgoing tide, we would be allowed to swim out to the reef.

'But only as far as the reef. No further. And when you get there, put your feet down so I can see that you're still in your depth.'

'To the rock! To the rock!' we would clamour, not really wanting it, being scared of it, but testing the adults. Just testing. 'Please, Poppa, please,' tugging at our grandfather's sleeve. 'Why can't we?'

'Because I'm in charge.'

In a sense the reef was an arbitrary marker because when the tide was up you couldn't really see it, just a line of riffs over a sandbar which was the last strip of sand to disappear when the tide was coming in. The current swirled over it and brought the tide in fast, so that if you got left out there (and only day visitors ever did) the siren would go from the coastguard, and a boat or a helicopter would be sent out. We would watch from the beach with a mixture of excitement and fear and foolish pride. For, of course, we knew better.

On an outgoing tide the reef turned the bay into a basin of safe swimming, a sort of lagoon. Beyond it was a rock, the Darras, a single tall stack with a hole through the middle and if you got out to the Darras you were in open water and you could swim through the hole and round the headland into the next bay. We had seen children do it, bigger children than us, serious swimming children with badges on their costumes and rubber caps. We had seen them disappear through the rock and later, much later, when they were sure to have been drowned, come running down the hill, down the red earth path of the grassy hill and back into our bay, jumping and punching the air with both hands. Look at us. We swam to St. Trewin's Cove. S'easy.

We swam early, before breakfast, when my grandparents came down from Liskeard to look after us and my parents returned to our home in

Scotland, and to their work. It was the part of the summer we liked best, for our grandparents came to their task with a Swallows and Amazons enthusiasm and it seemed to us boys quite natural that grandparents should somehow come up younger than parents. They didn't think much of reading books, or beach games, or tea in the garden, or introducing us to other children. What they liked was picnics and expeditions and marching along with haversacks on our backs, and whistling (my father never whistled) and climbing and looking for pirate caves and coming back to the cottage in the evening too tired for baths or teeth-cleaning but with just enough energy for sausages and baked beans and a couple of hands of racing demon.

That morning, the morning it happened, had been the same as any other. Except that Harry may have said, pulling on grandfather's hand as we skipped down to the beach, '*I* could do it. I'm the oldest. I'm the best swimmer.' He may have said it. Or he may not. Sometimes he did. Just say it. It didn't mean anything. He knew Poppa didn't allow.

And that morning, when we had stood up on the sand bar and turned and waved to Poppa, he may have swum a little way away from Jack and me, doing his crawl which he had just learnt. He hadn't got it right, there was a lot of rolling about in it, but he liked Poppa to look at it, standing watching us on the beach. He may have done that, or he may not. I don't know. All I know, all Jack and I knew, was that after we had swum through each other's legs six or seven times we got bored and wanted two pairs of legs to swim through, so we shouted for him to come and make another arch and he didn't come.

I don't remember when we began to panic, when the fear began to rise in our throats because: might not he have gone in before us, have got cold or something, and run back to the cottage? But when Poppa called him, then us, and we had swum quickly in to him, we saw his face. He was standing thigh-deep in the water and he said: 'Did he swim to the Darras? Did you see him go?' speaking very loudly, his face close to ours, and gripping our shoulders. We started to cry and he struck out into the water with all his clothes on and we stood shaking and crying at the water's edge. I don't know how long we were there but when he came out he panted: 'Get a towel round you, you stupid boys!' and he ran, with great wet strides, back to the cottage and we followed, stumbling and weeping in our bare feet, our shoes left behind on the beach.

Poppa was out all day, with neighbours and villagers and police and dogs. An RAF helicopter and a lifeboat had been sent for. Sometime in the afternoon Poppa came back, I think to see if we had news, and then he went out again taking us with him because he could see our minds could not be kept off it. He told Gran he would keep us well back, he wouldn't let us see. He meant the body, of course, should it have been washed up, but he needn't have bothered because it never was. Not that day, not weeks, not months later. Not there, in the bay, nor further up the coast, which is what might have been expected. The coastguards had never heard of such a thing, not in all their years of watching that coast.

We were on the news that night, but I don't think we saw it because Gran took us into the kitchen and made a point of talking, so that we heard only snatches. Three boys. Same family. Ten-year-old boy. Missing. Poppa was watching but after a while he must have turned it off because he came into the kitchen and when Gran said, 'Any news?' he shook his head and took down the big torch and put on his overcoat. We went up to bed and Gran came with us and got, fully clothed, into Harry's bed which was a proper bed, he being the eldest, and when we got out of our bunks and crept in beside her, cold with crying, she told us that there were lots of people out there, neighbours and local people and fishermen in boats, and Poppa too, and they would carry on searching, all through the night. It seemed strange to us that there should be all those people out there but we couldn't hear them. Only the sea.

Our parents drove through the night from our home in Inverness and when they reached us it was the morning of the following day, and there had been two tides. We had been waiting for them, running in and out of the picket-fenced front garden, and we saw the Rover coming along the beach road, my father behind the wheel, very white, my mother's face red and blotched.

She jumped out of the car and hugged the breath out of us and then we were in the cottage and I think our mother was hysterical because she was screaming at our grandfather, pounding his chest with clenched-up fists. He stood there, tall, square, rigid in his faded coral trousers and old Guernsey, his arms hanging loose by his sides. We heard the words: Blame. Trust. Stop it. Don't. And then: *Your* parents. *Your* father. I don't think our mother ever called grandfather Poppa after that day.

Our grandmother had made cups of tea. She brought one in and offered it to our mother who pushed it away and she turned and took it back into the kitchen, her hands shaking.

'Gran. Gran.' We ran after her and threw our arms around her aproned waist and sobbed into the stale, familiar cooking smells and the three of us stood there, held together by fear.

'Boys. Come back here.' Our mother's voice, shrill and harsh, seemed to belong to someone else. 'Go upstairs and pack your things. We're going home.'

Our grandmother, an arm round each of us, had brought us back into the sitting room and we watched our father take our mother by the shoulders and say her name, again and again: Mary. Mary. Mary. He pressed her shoulders as if trying to squeeze something out of her and then he moved her to one of the big old armchairs, its cover torn and springs gone from a hundred holiday lets and she sat down in it, suddenly. And then there were more words: Now. Later. Soon. Police. And a word I had not heard before but I know now must have been Witnesses.

'Witnesses,' my mother said. 'They're little boys.'

Next morning our parents took us down to the beach for the last time, not to swim but, I suppose, to say goodbye. After five tides, my parents had been advised not to hope, though how hope could be turned off was something we children could not understand, expecting at any moment that he might come running down the hill and on to the beach, punching the air. We stood in a row and held hands and my father mumbled something, it must have been a prayer. A helicopter whirred up the tideline, its insect tail low. When our mother drove us away, some hours later, it had turned and was headed down the coast. 'Wrong way! Wrong way!' I cried out in anguish from the back of the car. But my mother yanked the engine into another gear and accelerated up the hill and out of the little town.

Who knows what did, or didn't happen in childhood. So much of it is story. But that we were there, and still don't know, is what belays the night, when the pipes are cold and the street light raw outside our bedroom window, and my own children are sleeping close at hand and far away, tumbling in dreams.

'Because I'm in charge.' I can hear his voice now. And am for racing into the cold morning waves with the tide running and the current pulling, breasting the shock of the first immersion, turning to wave at him standing there, watching us. Knowing that we were safe.

NAUSICAA

Just a slight thickening of the waist. Nothing to worry about. The stomach was still flat, the bottom firm. The thighs ... the thighs were good. At any age a man's thighs are a better proposition than a woman's. For all her swimming and stretching and comparative youth, Marion could not compete below the waist. He turned sideways to the mirror and drew up the muscles of his pelvic floor. Not bad. Not bad at all.

'Another glass of wine, Jerome?'

'I think not, Owen, thank you.'

'Oh come now. This is supposed to be a literary lunch.'

'I thought they went out years ago.'

'In theory, yes. In practice we are allowed to push the boat out every now and again. Depending on the value of the catch.'

'You already have me in the net. I can't imagine I'm worth a large outlay.'

'You don't know what it is we want you to do.'

Jerome stopped eating, and put down his knife and fork. He took the white napkin from his lap and carefully wiped the corners of his mouth. Something in his publisher's tone discomfited him.

'It doesn't sound as if I'm going to like it,' he said. 'You'd better tell me what it is.'

'I won't do it,' he said, as he stood before his much younger partner, naked except for his underpants. 'It's in my contract. No signing sessions, no personal publicity, no TV, no chat shows.'

'It's hardly a chat show,' Marion said, undressing. 'And you know very well none of that stuff is in your contract. No publisher would agree to it. *I* certainly wouldn't. It's a contract in your head.'

'It was a verbal agreement. Between Hill Hopkins and me. I remember quite clearly outlining my conditions to Richard Hopkins in the early days.'

'Richard Hopkins is dead and the company has moved on. And so, my love, if I may say so, should you. The attitude you adopt doesn't sell any books. Authors belong to their readers today. I thought everyone knew that. Even J.K Rowling came to it eventually.'

'And much good it did her.'

'Anyway you know you've got to do it because if you don't they'll get that whatsisname from UEA, you know, the one you don't like.'

'Gay Warnham.'

'Yes, him.'

'It's a her. And she's a fraud.'

'Published?'

'A few papers. She's got a book coming out this Autumn.'

'Same time as yours?'

'I expect so.'

'There you are. You have no choice. You've got to do it.'

'I shouldn't have to. After thirty years in academic research, I am the recognised authority on James Joyce's *Ulysses* in the English-speaking world.'

'For how long?' Marion said.

'Bitch,' he said. He opened the button of her silk pyjama bottoms and they fell to the floor. 'Your thighs are fat.'

'Fat is sexy,' she said.

The table at *Rules* had been booked for twelve noon because Americans like to eat early, a fact which in itself had annoyed Jerome Le Fanu. He arrived at his publishers in Covent Garden at twelve fifteen, to be told that Owen Hill had already walked over to the restaurant. Jerome was therefore in a high temper when eventually he joined them, folded into the velvet, banquette accommodation and drinking Martinis. His intended TV adversary was a small, Jewish East Coast academic of about thirty-two years of age. Too young, thought Jerome. Too young and too Jewish to know anything about *Ulysses*, quickly correcting himself on the second count. He looked a bit like Woody Allen. Jerome sat down heavily opposite them. Oh God, let him not be funny, he thought. Please God, let him not be funny.

Owen effected the introductions. The small American, Larry J. Henkman, professed himself overwhelmed to meet a writer and scholar he had admired for so long and who had made such a contribution to the reading of Joyce. They had corresponded - did Professor Le Fanu remember? - over the *Nausicaa* chapter, when Henkman was writing his Ph.D. thesis. No, Jerome did not remember - he got so many Ph.D. students writing to him - but he certainly knew of Dr. Henkman's ('Larry, please') of ... Larry's reputation. He was delighted to meet him, he finished sulkily.

Larry J. Henkman, peering at the menu through small, horn-rimmed spectacles, ordered a fillet steak, rare, with fries, and said he thought the TV debate a fine idea. Jesus, on his side of the pond you only got that sort of programme on the educational channel. The BBC was so enlightened. Okay, okay, so it wasn't perfect, but hey, you've probably got to be an American to realise how lucky you are. Jerome enquired about the projected format. He felt trapped.

'It's a debate.' Owen paused as the waiter waited for him to taste the wine. 'Between the two of you. It ties in with a symposium U.C.L. is organising in the Autumn and, of course, with the publication of your new book, Jerome. The question briefly is: how accessible is *Ulysses* to the ordinary reader. Can it be enjoyed as straightforward narrative, or does it require a background of classical scholarship?'

'Presumably the latter, or we'd all be out of a job.'

'Well, that's what you will argue, and Larry will take the Everyman position. The debate will be chaired by someone like Melvyn (his listeners said 'Who?' and 'Oh God' simultaneously) and they will cut to actors reading passages and to ordinary people - Dubliners probably - who have read it.'

'That will be novel,' Jerome remarked drily. 'I don't think I've ever come across anyone who has just picked it up and read it. It's hardly Paddington to Temple Meads material.'

'That's where I will take issue with you, Professor. They would, if it was just sitting there on the bookstall with, like, a hot picture of Bella Cohen on the cover. It's we academics who get in the way of that. We stand between Joyce and the reader.'

'Oh God,' Jerome said wearily. He refilled his wine glass and that of Owen and held it over Henkman's, who covered his quickly with his hand. 'You realise you're cutting off your nose to spite your face?'

'Oh, it's only a piece of fun,' Henkman said. 'We shouldn't take it too seriously. It's just, like, a late-night intellectual ball game. Minor league, you know.'

'I am considered major league,' Jerome said stiffly, managing a smile.

'Of course, of course.' Owen had cut in quickly. 'We all know that. Look, Jerome, if you really don't think you can do it. I mean, we could always try to get ...'

'Of course I can do it. The question is, whether I choose to.'

'I met your little American today,' Marion said, reaching in the fridge for the white wine. 'I thought he was cute.'

'Cute,' Jerome said. 'Cute is exactly what I don't want to be pitched against. How did you meet? You're not going to publish him, surely?'

'No. He came over here, earlier this evening. He telephoned first. He wanted to have a look at your new book and Owen hadn't any in the office. He knew we had a pile of advance copies here, so he sent him over.'

'You didn't let him have one?'

'Of course. I thought you'd want me to. He's a huge fan.'

'Of yours, no doubt.'

'Of yours, silly. He's no slouch himself, from what I gathered. He's published quite a lot along the same lines as you - language, subtext, classical imagery. You should read him. In fact, you really *should* read him before you do that programme.'

'I can't read every minor academic who sets himself up as a Joycean expert. The world is full of them.'

'I know. But I think he's probably good. Very good. He told me you were his role model.'

'Then what the hell is he playing at?'

He had decided on a royal blue shirt, open at the neck, and charcoal tweed jacket but before make-up had finished with his face he was already regretting the blue.

'I don't want to look *tanned*,' he said to the mirror and the woman in it, who was applying more colour with a wet sponge. 'I don't want to look like a chat show host.'

'You're nothing like a chat show host,' she said. 'Much more distinguished. And better looking,' she added quickly.

'I should hope so.'

'But the lights tend to drain all the colour from the face. What may look a bit over-the-top here will appear quite natural before the camera. Trust me,' she said, touching his shoulder before turning to go.

'I have no choice.' He looked at his colourful face and admired, briefly, his thick crop of steel-grey hair. He put his hand up to touch it, and realised that he was shaking. He was also sweating. Christ, it was hot. It would be even hotter in the studio. What, in God's name was he doing here? He had never intended to do this. It wasn't his thing. He had never ... he reached in his pocket for his hip flask, unscrewed the stopper and took a swig. That was better. Much better. Where was he? Never intended ... his contract said ... his contract. He took another gulp. Then another. He pulled back his shoulders and straightened up. Get a grip, Le Fanu. You can do this. You can do this standing on your head. You have lectured to hundreds (another gulp), thousands (another long gulp) possibly *millions* (he tipped his head back and poured the remaining liquid into his mouth) of students in your life. But hang on a minute. He picked up a glass from the table in front of him and shook the few last drops into it. This is not a lecture. This is ... what is this? Thiss iss . thississ a confron ... confron ... mightaswellsuckthedamnthingdry ...

'Professor Le Fanu? Time.'

They stood around in a bleak ante-room clutching glasses of sparkling white and the producer and Lord Bragg pumped hands and expressed thanks and said it had all gone very well and as he tried to steady himself he saw across the room that Marion was involved in all sorts of body language and eye contact with Dr. Larry Henkman.

'Between ourselves,' he overheard, as he made his way heavily towards them, 'I doubt that we'll be able to use it. He was frightful.' Yes, he probably was frightful, that jumped-up little American. He was a frightful little prick. He must remember to tell him so.

'I think I'll take a rain check,' he said, reaching them. He leaned over Marion's shoulder to shake Henkman's hand. 'Goodnight,' he said. 'And before I forget, there's something I have to tell you. What was it? Oh yes, that's it. I have to tell you that you are a frightful little ...'

'Go home,' Marion said. 'Go back to the flat.'

'I'm going,' he said. 'Coming?' He swayed against her, his arm around her waist. She took it away and turned to him brightly.

'Sure,' she said. 'Later.'

Under the thick make-up, he looked decidedly off-colour. It came off in great pink streaks on to his flannel, but with difficulty. Probably he would need cream to remove it all. Marion would have some. Why wasn't she here? She could have done it for him. He wandered out of the bathroom towards her dressing table. Here they all were, the potions of eternal youth. She wasn't a pretty woman but she was vain and she was - sometimes he liked to calculate it, just now didn't seem like such a good idea - she was nearly twenty years younger than him. Probably he should have married her after the divorce, when she had wanted it. He picked up a jar of cleansing cream and sat in front of her mirror, rubbing extravagant handfuls into his face. He pulled out a bunch of tissues and wiped it off. He'd seen her doing something like this a hundred times. He peered towards the mirror. What now? His face looked very greasy. As if he'd just been sick. Cleanse and tone. Cleanse and tone. That was what she sat there chanting, from her beauty perch, as he lay in bed, waiting for her. What did it mean? He fumbled about among the jars and bottles. Toning

Lotion. That looked the ticket. He poured some on to a pad of tissues and rubbed vigorously, bringing some life back into his face. That was better. Beginning to look more like his old self.

Where was she? He glanced at the clock. Twelve-thirty. She ought to be back by now. Perhaps she'd left a message on the Answerphone when he was being brought home in the taxi. He checked. Nothing. She must be back soon. He needed to talk to her. He needed to know how he'd come over. It wasn't his sort of thing, he'd done it against his better judgement, but on the whole he felt ... how did he feel? Pleased with himself? He found he couldn't remember much of the interchange but yes, he could probably feel pleased with himself. He'd put on a pretty good show, he felt sure. He always did.

He clasped his hands above his head and stretched. He was still in pretty good nick. Just a slight thickening of the waist. Nothing to worry about. She'd be back any minute.

LAST RIGHTS

In stories, the husband often gets off lightly: confesses an affair, requests a divorce ... and gets thrown out. She doesn't want to throw him out. What she wants is to be told that this isn't happening, that she isn't losing what she loves most in the world. But she is hurt, betrayed and angry and in her anger she hurls herself into the scale and throws him out, and in that moment his affair is somehow ratified and their separation assured.

But she had not thrown him out. She had stood in the hall with her arms around his neck, pressing her forehead into his chest.

'No, Paul, no. Don't go. Please don't go. I love you.' So that in the end he had taken her hands and prised her arms apart, slipping down and out of her embrace, closing the door quietly behind him. She heard the start of the engine, the familiar gear changes as he manoeuvred the car out of its parking space and drove away.

All night she sat by the phone, crying, waiting for his call, waiting for it not to be true, the words 'I never meant to hurt you' hanging in the air against her hope. He had always been solicitous, calling to let her know where he was, if he needed supper, if he was going to be late. When Lucy was a baby, an exhausting, colicky baby, he had phoned her every day. 'Every day,' his colleagues had been incredulous, 'such devotion.' She couldn't go to bed, their bed. She would sell it, get a new one, get a duvet, as she had always wanted. A duvet, she thought bitterly. What did it matter, now.

How had it happened? When had it happened? Had there been a moment when she might have intuited, prevented? She couldn't remember a time when things had suddenly been different, or when he had seemed distant, or evasive, or even displeased with her. He had not stopped kissing her when he came in, or drawing her to him in the morning, or even making love. She shuddered. Where is it honed, this talent to deceive? In early years, in school? In little daily rituals of subterfuge? 'I've been trying to find the right moment.' 'I promised

Jessany I would tell you tonight.' She saw his drawn face, the anguish in his eyes, the pleading to be understood, forgiven, helped. God, she had been so angry. That he should do all this to her and still, somehow, seek her blessing. He was weak, weak and childish, stupid and vain and he had been trapped. Yes, that was it, trapped. As her fancy rolled on in that direction, her reason caught up with it and dragged it back and she thought of the cold bed upstairs and a warm one somewhere else and she tried, and tried not, to understand.

She would fight. She would go into chambers tomorrow and talk to David. He would be shocked, she knew. She would demand that he sack her. Or find her another pupillage, on the understanding that she break off the affair with Paul. Could he do that, she wondered? Well, he would have to. Otherwise she would go to the *Mail* and the *Sun* and the *Express* and the *News of the World* and drag Mr. Paul Henderson and the chambers of Sir David Ingram-Hill, Q.C. through the dirt, knowing, as she thought it, that she would not. As dawn brought into definition the pale contours of the garden she recalled that the last time she had gone through a night without sleep was at a May Ball, thirty-two years ago, with Paul.

At some time in the morning she telephoned her secretary, protesting a high fever and asking for some manuscripts to be sent over by cab. She couldn't imagine reading them or even looking at them, but she knew that her job was going to be her lifeline, her sanity. She made herself a cup of tea - she had had nothing to eat or drink except whisky for nearly twenty-four hours - phoned her doctor for an appointment that evening and slept fitfully through the day, waking only to cry, to take the taxi delivery, to switch on the Answerphone, to cry again. She couldn't face talking to anyone, not even her closest friends, and she was going to the doctor only because she had run out of sleeping pills. Also, she did not want to be in the house when Paul came back for his things.

The doctor was reluctant to prescribe pills without good reason. She had been determined not to break down, but as he leaned towards her sympathetically she felt her eyes filling with tears and great sobs forced themselves up into her throat. Finally she pulled herself together. 'My mother is dying,' she lied, looking away. He might find, if he checked her notes, that her mother was dying for the second time.

Despite her best efforts, Paul was in the drawing room when she returned. Cases and grips were piled up neatly by the front door. He had obviously arrived by taxi, and planned to leave that way. He was moving uneasily around the room, touching books, pulling out CDs and pushing them quickly back again.

'I don't suppose ...no... I shouldn't really take these. They give you pleasure too.'

'Oh, pleasure. My pleasure. Suddenly my pleasure is important, is it? How can you talk like that?' She took out the C.D. he had replaced and flung it across the room. 'How can you imagine that ... that a bloody Brandenburg is going to make any difference when ...' she faced him, 'when everything I love is walking away from me. Paul, I love you. I've never stopped loving you. Don't do this. Please. Don't go.'

He sank wearily on to the sofa. 'This isn't easy for me either. You know I love you too, in my way. But this thing with Jessany. I have to be with her. I need her. She ...'

'Don't say she makes you feel young', she flared.

'No. I wasn't going to. In fact she makes me feel older. Protective. Needed. She needs me.'

'And I don't?'

'You're strong. You'll be all right.'

'How the hell do you know? And what about Lucy? Will she be 'all right' as you so smugly put it?'

'She's twenty-eight.'

'So?'

'She's old enough to understand.'

'To understand that her father, her adored father, has just decided to take a mistress only slightly older than herself? Or perhaps she's younger? *Is* she younger? Just how old is this ... woman? Not that I give a damn.'

'She's .... twenty-seven.'

'Oh God. Oh God, Paul. Look at yourself. Just look at yourself. You're fifty-five years old. You're nearly thirty years older than she is. How long can you possibly expect it to last? A year? Two? Women who go for married men don't usually stop at one.'

He looked up at her bleakly. 'It's a risk I'm going to have to take. I love her, Jane. I fell in love with her. I didn't mean to, but I did. There's nothing to be done.'

She gazed at him. Then, disgusted, she turned away. 'You are pathetic. Pathetic and nauseating. It's contemptible. It's ... almost obscene.'

He went on, apparently unheeding. It was as if, having found sufficient momentum, his words were following one upon another in some pre-programmed form and he was neither their originator nor their purveyor. They were just words, coming out into the room to be caught, like bubbles, and somehow related to her life. She heard 'solicitor' and 'divorce' and 'settlement' and she knew that these bubble-words would destroy her.

'I can't'. she said. Can't what, she thought. Can't accept, understand, cope, respond? 'I can't bear it.'

'You'll be all right.' For the second time this confident, arrogant assumption, although this time it seemed to be addressed less to her than to himself. Then he rose, as if from a difficult board meeting, and began to walk briskly round the room, drawing the proceedings to a close, wrapping things up. 'So. I think it best to keep things to ourselves for the moment. At least until I've had a chance to tell David. No-one in chambers knows or even suspects.' He caught her glance. 'No, really. We've been discreet. And of course there's Lucy. I must talk to her before anyone else. I think I'll ring her and see if I can't go round to her flat tomorrow evening.'

'Oh no. You're not getting off that lightly. You're not having the luxury of a cosy little chat with Lucy on your own. You can talk to her here, in this house, in front of me, in front of both of us.'

'You won't use her against us?' The 'us' that was no longer herself and Paul came over her like sickness.

'I won't need to.' She was glad. Glad and infinitely sorry for the hurt he was about to inflict on their daughter. They had been through so much with her. And now, when happiness and stability seemed within her grasp... 'she's going to feel betrayed.'

'Betrayed? She hasn't been betrayed.'

'She has. Not in the same way as I have, but betrayed nonetheless. She counts on us being there, for her and for each other. As we always have been. And now you'll be there for someone else.'

'I'll always be there for Lucy.'

'It won't be the same. How can it? And don't you realise, she has *no idea*. She can have no idea that this is happening in our lives, in her life.'

It was a myth promulgated by novels from publishing houses like her own that those in the throes of great passion produce some sort of antibody that inhibits its effect. The reality was different. They can be set in amber, their centre can hold. But all around them, things fall apart.

'I don't know how I'm going to tell her.'

'I'm sure you'll find a way. You did with me. Hurting people gets progressively easier, so I'm told.'

'But I love her so much.'

'Do you,' she said. She walked into the kitchen.

She heard his key turn in the lock and she was on her own again. He had double-locked the door behind him, out of habit, as if the house was empty, as if, for him, she had ceased to exist.

Lucy phoned her during the evening to see if she wanted to go to a play later in the month. 'It's Strindberg. I don't think it's quite Dad's cup of tea, do you?'

They had always laughed about Paul's taste in entertainment, Paul as much as the two of them. 'No. No. Best not ask him.'

'What's the matter? You sound ghastly. As a matter of fact, you sound slightly pissed.' She laughed.

'I've got a cold. I haven't been in to the office today. They sent round some manuscripts and I've been reading them over a large whisky. I haven't had anything to eat yet.'

'What? It's ten o'clock. You'd better get yourself something now, as soon as I've put the phone down. Is Dad back?'

'No.'

'Good God. It's terribly late.'

'I know. But you know what he's like. He's ... got a big case coming up in Strasbourg.'

'What it is to be a fancy Euro-lawyer. Do you think he'll ever be a judge?'

'I really don't know,' she said wearily.

'Okay, okay. I get the picture. You're tired, you want to go to bed. But get something to eat first, right? You know your trouble, Mum. You play the martyr too much. Me and Dad are always saying that. Look, I'll probably pop over at the weekend. Give my love to Dad. And can you tell him I think there's something wrong with the drive shaft on my car. Perhaps he'll take a look at it for me.'

'I don't know.'

'Of course he will. That's what he's there for, isn't it. Bye now then, Mum. Take care.' Almost immediately the phone rang again. 'And don't forget. *Get something to eat.*'

She didn't. And the combination of whisky and valium produced vivid, frightening dreams so that when she awoke, about five a.m., with raised heartbeat and clammy limbs, she was momentarily glad to be out of them. But the strange bed brought a much worse reality into her waking consciousness and she pushed aside the spare room bedclothes, wet with tears and perspiration, and made her way slowly downstairs to greet another empty dawn.

She thought she might be going mad. How long did it take to go mad? Confused phrases from church and childhood chased each other round in her head. *Truly and indifferently minister justice. And on the third day. Grant us thy peace.* Was this the third day? Or the second day? She found that she couldn't remember. It felt like the third day. And on the third day God created ... and Paul destroyed. No, that was the first day. The first day was the day of destruction. And after that there was no justice and no peace. Lack of food was a contributory factor, she knew. She must try to eat some breakfast. As she laid the tray, she longed. Longed for someone to care for, for her mother, for their old dog. She longed for Paul.

'Mrs. Henderson?' The voice of Geoffrey, the chambers' chief clerk, caused her to draw her dressing-gown more tightly around her and adjust her position by the telephone. 'Mrs. Henderson. I have Sir David on the phone for you. And may I just say, Mrs. Henderson. I'm so very sorry. We all are.'

Oh God, she thought. If Geoffrey knows, everyone knows. I can't handle it. Why should I have to? What business of theirs is it anyway? It's a private matter, private. I don't have to discuss it with Sir David Ingram Bloody-Hill. Why should I? I shan't speak to him. I shall...

'Jane. David. Jane, something terrible has happened. I wish there was some other way of telling you ...'

'Oh, don't bother about me. I'm sure you have nothing to say that I don't already know.'

'I'm sorry? Look, Jane. I don't think you understand. There's been an accident.'

'Accident?'

'Yes, an accident. Well, a heart attack. Paul has had a heart attack.'

'Heart attack?'

'Yes.'

'Where?'

'Here. In chambers.'

'When?'

'A few minutes ago. We've called an ambulance - ah, it's here now. Thank you, Geoffrey.'

'Which hospital?'

'Which hospital, Geoffrey? Thank you. The London.'

'I'm on my way.'

'Jane. Jane dear. They ... we ... we don't think he's going to make it.'

She arranged the funeral for the following Saturday. 'I'm so glad you did, Jane.' Joel Playfair, a glass of wine in one hand, was leaning towards her, speaking in a low, earnest voice against the strange, controlled hubbub of her drawing room. 'It meant we could all be here, you know. We generally find it so awfully difficult to get away for this sort of ...' he broke off embarrassed. 'Now *this* young lady,' he grabbed the arm of a young woman who had entered the room with a colleague, 'didn't want to come, not knowing you, and new to chambers, you know. But I insisted on it, positively insisted. One hundred per cent turnout for Paul, I said. Even Geoffrey and his merry men are here, you know. Oh, forgive me', he released the woman's arm. 'This is Jessany Marshall, our latest bright young thing. Jessany, Mrs. Henderson, Paul's wife.'

'How kind of you to come.'

She was short, nervous, with small features and steel-framed glasses. 'Oh, not at all, not at all. Mrs. Henderson ...' Jane saw that behind the glasses, the eyes had filled with tears.

'Of course, of course. All Paul's colleagues were devoted to him.' She turned, as if to move away. Joel drew her back.

'To you both, my dear. To you both. You were such a ... couple. We all felt it. Envied him, you know.' He put his arm round her shoulders. 'He was a happy man, Jane, a happy man. Remember that, my dear, when things seem insurmountable, as they must. Well now. I shall pop round to see you in a day or two. Or perhaps you'd allow an old friend to take you to dinner? That is, if it's not too soon ...'

'No. I'd like that, Joel. Really I would. Thank you.'

Lucy came down from the bathroom. She had been crying, and was walking towards her angrily across the suddenly silent room. 'Mum. All Dad's stuff. His shaving things...' She looked quickly round the room, taking in with relief the family photographs in their old places, on the piano, the tables, the mantelpiece. She took down a favourite, of her father and herself at her twenty-first party, their heads close, laughing together in the old familiar way. The tears rolled off her face and on to the glass.

'I'm sorry. I thought you'd ... got rid of everything. I understand about the shaving things. But you won't put the photographs away, will you, like some women do when their husbands ... you know... as if they had never ... you won't do that, will you?'

She held her sobbing daughter in her arms. Then she took the photograph from her hands and, wiping it gently with her sleeve, replaced it carefully on the mantelpiece, among its companions, where it belonged.

CHINA DOLL

There were no dolls in our home. No dolls and no guns. Our mother, exposed to the writings of Simone de Beauvoir at an impressionable age, took the view that gender is a matter not of birth, but of experience. And so we were experiments, my brother and I, *tabulae rasae*, born neither male nor female, awaiting the imprint of life.

Our birthday presents, as I recall, were largely educational. Toy garage forecourts where the pumps worked, supermarkets where the tills registered, puzzles, learning games. Once, *distrait*, Papa arrived at the flat with a doll. Through the cellophane I caught a glimpse of the wax face, the pink net dress, the golden curls before - '*Ça non, alors*' - Maman snatched it away. '*Tu as oublié*,' she said.

In general, the toys were shared. I knew, from an early age, the gauge of the tracks of our Jouef model railway, and how to change the points at the last minute, sending the engine off on another set of rails, away from where Sacha was expecting it. The small living room of our apartment at number forty-nine Rue de la Tourelle was our playroom. Sometimes our mother watched us, making notes. She was working on a paper, published now but never read by us, under the title *Problems of Gender in a Post-Feminist Society.*

Papa did not live with us and could not marry our mother, having already a family of his own. He visited once a week, usually on Saturday. Since he was head of the department in which our mother worked, Maman must necessarily be used to seeing him, yet she was tense before his arrival, sometimes changing into a skirt but still managing to look more or less the same. She set out a bottle of red wine and two glasses and after he had played with us a little they sat together and she talked a great deal, very fast. Papa was not a young man, though his beard and slight stoop may have aged him in our eyes, and he often seemed quite tired when he rose to leave, although he had not moved.

They were rather modern, our domestic arrangements. Papa's wife, Magdalena, seemed fond of us and happy to absorb us into her family life when Papa wished. Our summers were spent at her country house at Fontainebleau, a tall, chateau-style villa with large rooms, high ceilings, deep windows and shutters. A formal, *parterre* garden separated the house from the river. It was Magdalena's delight, laid out with low box hedges in geometric shapes each surrounding a bay tree or standard rose. In the centre was a blue rose which, we were advised, Papa had presented to Magdalena on the first anniversary of their marriage. It was a symbol of their enduring love. A specialist grower had created the rose for her, and given it her name. No-one but Magdalena was allowed to touch it. The blooms were never cut, never brought into the house. The box hedges surrounding it, we were told, were to be run round, not jumped over. But how could four children racing to the river on a hot summer's day not jump over low box hedges? They were a little older than us, our half-sibling sister and brother. They called us *nos jumeaux blonds*. Our flaxen-haired twins.

Magdalena and Maman rarely met, though there seemed no enmity between them. In France, a mistress is neither a secret nor an object of pity. Perhaps the reverse, since our mother accompanied Papa to the theatre and to soirées and often announced herself on the telephone as the mistress of Georges Valencennes. She did not spend the month of August at Fontainebleau with us, not because she was not invited but because it was a time when she might pursue her research, and travel. '*Ta maman, elle est très intelligente, tres érudite,*' Magdalena said, as if it were an illness.

I do not know whether Magdalena was apprised of Maman's experiment in child-rearing. Possibly she was, and chose to ignore it. At all events our arrival at Fontainebleau each summer in matching jeans and shirts was greeted with the same degree of horror and we were sent upstairs - *vite*! - to find something more chic from the wardrobes of Gerard and Celeste. 'It is because your mother is an academic,' Magdalena explained. 'She has no time for these things.'

Magdalena had time for these things. Red-haired, long-limbed and elegant, she wore filmy clothes, and jewellery, and floated past us in a haze of Guerlain's *L'Heure Bleu*. When she followed through the garden to watch us swimming she stepped round, not over, the box hedges, shading her face from the sun with a lilac parasol. An old dinghy was our makeshift diving board. We plunged into the river from the rocking boat, swimming quickly back, heaving ourselves over the side to go straight in again. Sacha was the best diver, hurling himself out over the water way beyond where the rest of us could reach.

Magdalena watched from the shade of her parasol. *'Bravo, mon petit Sacha, bravo!'*

'Regarde-moi, Maman, regarde-moi,' Gerard cried.

'Oui, oui.' But it was Sacha who drew her admiration.

At the top of the house, under a mansard roof, was the bedroom I shared with Celeste and seven dolls. Exquisitely attired in the fashions of the late nineteenth century, the dolls' painted porcelain faces had full cheeks, high, arched brows and small tight mouths. The beauty was in their clothes, silk dresses perfect in every detail with lace and organza and miniature pearl buttons; bustles and *bustiers* and layers of petticoat stiffened with hoops; tiny shoes and gloves of kid; velvet hats and ivory-handled parasols trimmed with lace.

'Their clothes are by the most famous Paris couturiers,' Celeste said. 'Maman says they were made to teach young girls the secrets of grace and style, though I don't think you and I will have dresses as beautiful as these.' She stroked the stiff silk of a little skirt. 'They were given to Maman by her mother, and to grandmother by her mother, and to grandmother's mother ...' - Celeste wrestled briefly with the problem of genealogy - 'anyway now they are mine and I have named them all. I will introduce you. You mustn't mind that they seem so grand. I think they think they come from better families than we do. 'Now Mathilde,' she said, picking up a doll in a brown striped taffeta dress and matching cape, 'I would like you to meet Kira, my half-sister. You are to be very nice to her, and not *mechante*, and she will be good to you. We are allowed to play with them,' Celeste explained, 'but very carefully.'

Mathilde, Hortense, Suzanne, Lisette, Clara, Veronique and Amelie lived in the kneehole of a pretty little *escritoire* in Celeste's room. In the day they were brought out and arranged in various poses around the room. At night Celeste gathered them up and returned them to the *escritoire*, draping a curtain over the kneehole. Should she leave a chink of light through which the dolls might peep, I would slip out of bed and adjust the curtain.

'What are you doing?'

'Saying goodnight.'

'They have been said goodnight to. They are asleep by now. Get back into bed.'

We were playing in her room, Celeste and I, when we had what Gerard called the catastrophe of the bird shit. A sparrow came in through the open window. Panicked, it flew randomly around the room, ricocheting off walls and mirrors. It would not find the open window. Celeste ran out on to the landing to call Gerard and he came up, followed by Sacha and Magdalena. The sparrow had been eating purple berries and the consequences of its fear and indigestion were sprayed around the room. A quantity had spotted Amelie's grey taffeta dress. Magdalena scooped up the dolls and pushed them under the *escritoire*. The bird was now collapsed on the floor where it lay awkwardly, one wing spread out. Magdalena took a coat hanger from Celeste's wardrobe.

'The bird is injured, alas. It has no chance of survival. I fear it must be killed.'

Sacha stood between Magdalena and the bird. '*Non!*'

'His wing is damaged. I think he cannot fly.'

'*Non,*' Sacha said again.

Magdalena met his eyes, and suddenly threw down the hanger. 'Very well,' she said. She bent down and picked up the bird and walked to the window. Stretching out her arms she opened her cupped hands and after a moment the bird raised its wings and fluttered erratically away. 'Well, he must take his chances. Sometimes a quick death may be the better way.'

'I don't like it,' Sacha said.

'I know.' Magdalena knelt down and took his face in her hands. 'You have a beautiful soul, my little Sacha. That is why we love you.' She put her face to his blond head and kissed it lightly.

We cleaned up the room whilst Magdalena attended to the dolls. Amelie's dress was removed and sent to a dry cleaners in Paris and it was some time, Celeste said, before she was fully clothed again.

Amelie was the doll Celeste liked least, not simply because of the episode of the bird shit.

'She has very bad hair,' Celeste complained. It was real, but a bright shade of red. 'You have nice hair, Kira. Why don't we give her some of yours.'

We cut some hair from the ends of my pigtails and tucked it under her fine hat but it was not satisfactory, hanging down from the brim lank and straight, like the new hair that it was.

'Amelie, you are *not nice*,' Celeste said, stabbing a porcelain cheek with the little comb she had been using to arrange the hair. 'I cannot make you beautiful. I am going to give you to Kira, and then you'll be sorry.'

She took the doll by the legs and pushed her towards me.

'There. You have her. Don't you want her?'

'Well, but I am not allowed ...'

'Do you want her or not? Last chance.'

'Yes.'

Celeste fetched a brown box and packed Amelie into it with tissue paper. A little ashamed of herself by now, she folded back the tissue and kissed the doll and told her that she would miss her very much but that she was sure she would be happy in her new home. Then she pressed down the lid and handed the box to me.

'But don't tell Maman.'

She meant Magdalena, of course, though in truth neither Maman could be told.

Back in Paris, I showed my secret to Sacha.

'It's one of Celeste's. You have stolen it.'

'No. She gave her to me. She doesn't like her any more. She says she's mean and ugly.'

Sacha took the doll from the box and held her up. 'I don't think she's ugly. I think she's nice. We should call her Magdalena.'

We kept Magdalena under my bed, and the wonder was that Maman never found her.

When we were ten, our summers at Fontainebleau came to an end. Papa had taken an appointment at the university in Freiburg. The house at Fontainebleau, which belonged to Magdalena's family and not, as we had believed, to Magdalena herself, was to be sold. We arrived, that last summer, to packing cases and men in brown overalls, to rugs rolled up and labelled and pictures stacked against walls, to endless telephone instructions for Magdalena from Papa, and empty, echoing rooms. Only the minimum of furniture remained; a table and chairs, the cooker, our beds. In Celeste's room the dolls, deprived of their little home in the *escritoire*, lolled against the wall.

'They are very unhappy, poor dears. I think they are cross with me. But I am taking them with me. I have told them so. Maman is bringing up boxes and a special case to pack them in. I have told them all this. I wish they would not carry on so.'

She knelt down on the floor. 'We are moving to Germany, *mes petites*. It cannot be helped. Now go to sleep and pretend to be happy about it.' She placed a silk scarf carefully over them, and sighed, and sat on the bed. 'You are taking good care of Amelie?'

'Of course.' I did not think it tactful to tell her that Amelie had been re-named.

'Well, one day you will bring her to Freiburg and we will all be re-united. I expect she will be happier in Paris than in boring old Germany anyway.'

Also, in that summer, Magdalena lost her temper. The extent to which her temper had been lost was not at first apparent, for she was very quiet when she called us down to the hall and led us into the kitchen. She pointed to an arrangement of blue roses in the centre of the wooden table, although arrangement is hardly an appropriate description of the blooms which had been stuffed, apparently at random, into an old preserving jar. It was the jar the boys used when they went fishing in the river. The string still hung down from under the neck.

'Who did this?' she said. 'Who cut my roses?'

'I did,' Sacha said. He moved forward and touched the flowers with his hands, trying to urge them into a more appealing shape. 'For you.'

'No-one touches my roses, no-one. You know this. You know it.'

'I'm sorry. I'm sorry. I forgot.'

Magdalena looked at him, head drooping. For a moment it appeared as if she would relent. Then she took a step back, turned away and said, 'No, it won't do. I am very angry. Sacha, you will go home. Your mother will collect you.'

'But Maman…' Gerard reached for her hand.

'*Non.*'

'Please …'

'*Non.* My mind is made up.'

And so Sacha was sent home, and after several telephone calls it was decided that I should accompany him and when our mother came to collect us and swept us out of the house Magdalena found she could not leave whatever it was she was doing in another part of the house, and only the children saw us off. At home, I tried, although I did not fully understand it myself, to explain what had happened and Sacha left us and spent, I thought, a lot of time alone in his room.

Maman was pleased to have us back. We went to the park and to the playground, the three of us, Maman with her notebook.

We never went to Freiburg, but we heard about the children from time to time, when Papa visited. Gerard, we learnt, was scientific and would go to Heidelberg to study medicine. Celeste was a poetess, intense. She passed her *Abitur* at eighteen and at nineteen enrolled at the University of Freiburg.

Some time later, Magdalena left Papa. He had taken another mistress, a fellow student with Celeste, which Magdalena said was too much. She came to Paris and telephoned Maman about a doll we had, a doll which Celeste had lent to Kira once. Magdalena had brought to Paris Celeste's collection of dolls which she intended to have valued and catalogued and sold at auction. Fortunately Celeste had taken good care of her dolls. She hoped that Kira had done the same. She was on her own now, and could use the money.

Maman put down the telephone. 'She says it is a *Jumeau*, worth thousands. I told her I had no idea what she was talking about. We have no doll.'

'Well...' I said.

'Ah.' Maman had seen my face. 'Where is it?'

'In my room, I should imagine. It was under the bed. We used to play with it.'

'Sacha, be a dear and go and fetch it for us.'

'Kira can get it.'

Behind some clothes, at the back of a cupboard, I found the box. I pulled it out and blew the dust off and brought it to Maman. 'We haven't looked at it for years,' I said. I took off the lid.

Maman pulled back several layers of tissue paper and took out four dismembered limbs, a silk dress cut to shreds, a torso, a head.

'She has met a violent death,' Maman said, without emotion. 'I wonder why.'

She replaced the pieces carefully in the box and snapped on the lid.

MRS. PINKNEY AND THE WHEELIE-BIN

Mrs. Pinkney. Eighty-two years old. Stepping out through the village in her stout shoes and sensible skirt, stockings a little wrinkled at the ankle, quilted green jacket frayed and faded from a too intimate association with the washing machine. She is on her way to visit Mr. Cadbury, recently returned from hospital.

'My goodness, Mrs. Pinkney, you're looking well.' Mr. Gould, the organist.

'Thank you, Henry, thank you. Fighting fit. And yourself.' Mrs. Pinkney hurries on.

'Never ask people how they are,' Mr. Pinkney used to say, 'because they are more than likely to tell you.' Mrs. Pinkney, whilst honouring the maxims of her late husband, finds something not quite right about this one. She overcomes it by presenting a question as a statement. 'And yourself,' seems to answer all the requirements of good manners whilst at the same time drawing the respondent into a general aura of good health - her own good health. 'And it does them good,' she says.

Not as mobile as once she was, Mrs. Pinkney nevertheless gets around, drives a pale green Morris Minor and takes just half a beta-blocker a day for a bit of a dicky heart. ' You never hear her complain.' Margaret, in the village shop. Nor do you. 'Musn't complain' is a phrase Mrs. Pinkney particularly dislikes and never uses. If you mustn't, then don't.

Up the hill Mrs. Pinkney pants, the plastic bag handles cutting into the fingers of her right hand. She used to carry a basket but felt too much like a children's book illustration. She is taking Mr. Cadbury some plums. Every year she spends one very hot day bottling the yield of her fecund Victoria, later distributing around the village those jars which have not exploded. Mr. Cadbury will turn down the volume whilst she is there but as long as it is not during the last few furlongs he will not mind. Mrs. Pinkney will not stay long. She doesn't like to hang about.

Mr. and Mrs. Pinkney arrived in the village shortly after Mr. Pinkney's retirement. They met when Mr. Pinkney joined the firm of solicitors handling Mrs. Pinkney's father's estate. Mr. Pinkney had left a partnership and a first marriage in Redditch and moved into Leamington Spa and the orbit of Lavender, the farmer's daughter who, as she put it, scraped him off the floor, dusted him down and set him off on the right tack. 'He made a bad first marriage. People do. Mustn't hold it against them. In any case, I was the beneficiary, was I not? Got a husband and a son without any of the hazards of birth or breast-feeding.' 'Like a house on fire' is how she describes her relationship with Mr. Pinkney's son. And this is true, except that the flames burn at a distance since Robin has lived abroad for all but the first few years of his father's second marriage.

On retirement Mr. Pinkney found that he didn't have quite enough to do. Mrs. Pinkney found the same. So she set him off in his Volkswagen Passat to look at bungalows. The stairs in the Leamington Spa town house seemed to fornicate and multiply by the day. 'Sniffing around,' Mr. Pinkney called his activities and they provided diverting cocktail conversation for Mrs. Pinkney at the end of her day at the charity shop or the book club or the Friends of Queen Elizabeth Hospital. When he said he had seen a nice one at Pinkney's Green, she set down her gin and tonic.

'Where, did you say?'

'Pinkney's Green.'

'Where's that?'

'North of Stratford. Just off the A439.'

'Specifications?'

'Four bedrooms, 2 bathrooms, double garage. Set back from the main road by a gravel drive of about thirty yards.'

'Same spelling? Pinkney with an 'i'?'

Mr. Pinkney nodded.

'Well,' Mrs. Pinkney said. 'Well. It must be meant.'

Mrs. Pinkney has a rough, cheerful complexion and hard grey hair which she has washed and set in Stratford once a week. 'Frightful expense, but worth every penny.' That this is true is debatable. The phrase 'bad hair day' is probably unknown to Mrs. Pinkney but it would adequately describe almost any day in the Pinkney coiffure cycle. It has gone quite flat by the time she has puffed her way to Mr. Cadbury's front door.

Mr. Cadbury's horse has just come in second in the 3.30 at Plumpton. This is a source of immense dissatisfaction since, as he is explaining to Mrs. Pinkney, 'I only backed the bugger to win.'

Mrs. Pinkney agrees that it is disappointing and sets down her jar of plums on the television. These days people simply don't try hard enough.

'Pulled, more like,' Mr. Cadbury says.

Mrs. Pinkney enquires what, if anything, Mr. Cadbury needs from the shop (he hands her an already prepared list) and whether he would like a lift to church on Sunday. Mr. Cadbury says he'll see, he's sort of had it with the Almighty at the moment.

'I'll tell you what I don't need, Mrs. P. And that's a bleeding Wheelie-bin.'

He passes Mrs. Pinkney a clutch of papers he has received from the Council's Environmental and Operational Services Department. They announce a change in refuse collection. In accordance with EU Health and Safety regulations, household waste will no longer be taken away in plastic bags. Instead, every householder will be issued with a Wheelie-bin. These will be collected, as before, on Thursdays, from the point of the householder's property which abuts the main road. Householders will find that Wheelie-bins are both eco- and user-friendly. For those who would like to attend, demonstrations will take place in designated villages. Each householder will be informed when their Wheelie-bin service is due to commence.

Mrs. Pinkney hands back the papers with a snort.

'Yours not arrived then?'

'No. I'm not having one.'

'You are,' he says.

Mrs. Pinkney has no friends. What she has is chums. Old chums, new chums, village chums, professional chums, gardener chums, plumber chums and small chums. Her small chums, other people's children, come to her when their mothers need to visit an elderly relative or keep a hospital appointment. 'I stand no nonsense and take no prisoners', she cries, shooing them into her house with a clap of her hands. Quite what is meant by this curious announcement no-one knows, but the children run in happily and to date none has gone missing.

When Mrs. Pinkney arrives home she finds that her gardener chum has been. He has mown the lawn and cut back the shrubs. He is sorry (she finds a note under the flower pot) that he has not been able to find the wire coat hanger Mrs. Pinkney says she dropped in the driveway. Mrs. Pinkney will forgive him, but his eyes are not what they were. What he has done is to wheel the Bin the Council delivered while you was out round the back and leave it by the back door. He trusts this is satisfactory. His postscript advises that someone from the Council put the instructions for the Bin through the letterbox.

Mrs. Pinkney finds the instructions on the mat inside the front door. She tears them in two and throws them into the wastepaper basket.

Outside her back door she encounters her Bin, a large, green, upright plastic box on wheels. Smaller than an adult, bigger than a small boy. Paint a face on it and it would look like a small boy. William the Wheelie-bin, eco-warrior, comic-strip hero. Plucky and persistent, fighting the good fight against the detritus of rural life. 'Well don't imagine you're staying,' she tells it. 'Because you're not.'

Mrs. Pinkney wastes no time. She gets out her recently serviced Parker pen - 'if you want to keep a fountain pen running, you must treat it like a car' - shakes it once or twice to make sure the Quink Permanent Blue is flowing as freely and startlingly as she would wish, and begins.

She is eighty-three years old, she writes, anticipating her next birthday by several months. She lives on her own, drives a car, and on the whole manages pretty well. But what she cannot manage, what she has no intention of managing, is a thirty-yard haul over a loose gravel drive with a Wheelie-bin. She will continue to leave her rubbish in the usual place and the usual receptacle. The Council may take back the Wheelie-bin at their leisure. Mrs. Pinkney's handwriting, which is large, has grown larger. She signs off with a flourish.

In reply, Mr. Patrick of the Environmental and Operational Services Departrment, sends a very nice letter. This is the opinion of Mr. Patrick. Mrs. Pinkney's opinion is that it is a patronising letter and, which is more, one which completely misses the point. Mr. Patrick apparently understands Mrs. Pinkney's position and will send out one of his EcoAction Team, a Mr. Reemer, to personally introduce Mrs. Pinkney to her Wheelie-bin and explain the new system.

Mrs. Pinkney is on the telephone to a chum before the split infinitive can absorb any of her anger. She is waving the letter about in the air with her free hand.

'But they're quite easy to use, Lavender. If you don't understand the literature you can go to one of the demonstrations. You did get the literature?'

'I threw it in the bin.'

'In the Wheelie-bin?'

Mrs. Pinkney is not amused.

Mr. Reemer makes an appointment to visit Mrs. Pinkney on Friday afternoon. He looks forward to being able to demonstrate that it is quite possible for a lady such as herself to use a Wheelie-bin.

'And I look forward to demonstrating to you that it is not.'

Mrs. Pinkney spends much of Friday in unaccustomed indecision. Mr. Reemer is due at three o'clock. At two-thirty she resolves to move the Wheelie-bin. It would be better if it were to be found where it was left, by her front gate. To leave it where it is implies some sort of acceptance. She will say that she has not been able to drag it to her back door, not even empty. Good thinking. She grasps the handle.

'William, my boy. You're on your way.'

Mr. Reemer arrives at Mrs. Pinkney's at ten past three. To find ... what does Mr. Reemer find? Mrs. Pinkney dead? Mrs. Pinkney astride a Wheelie-bin flying out of the village and his sight? No. Mrs. Pinkney is a subject neither for tragedy nor magic realism. What Mr. Reemer finds is Mrs. Pinkney spreadeagled on the gravel and 'in a very bad way' as he reports back to headquarters on his mobile. He is told to call an ambulance at once.

Mrs. Pinkney is sitting up in bed in the private wing of the Queen Elizabeth Hospital. She has been taken down to X-ray and her left fibula is almost certainly fractured. The wire coat hanger on which Mrs. Pinkney tripped when making her historic Wheelie-bin run, and which she concealed from Mr. Reemer's eyes under her skirt, has been straightened out and hung in her hospital closet, inside a jacket.

Mrs. Pinkney accepts the cup of tea brought in by one of the Hospital Friends and pushes it to the corner of her bed table. She lays out the pen and the Basildon Bond which her cleaning lady chum has brought in. She waits, again, for the bright blue ink to flow and embarks on her second letter to Mr. Patrick of Environmental and Operational Services. Mrs Pinkney is in pain but content. She is about to embrace the compensation culture.

AMERICAN HOT

'Car wash?'

They stand outside her front door, laconic and unenthusiastic. She is irritated both by the interruption and the brevity of the address. 'Would-you-like-your-car-washed?' is six syllables, six seconds. Six seconds gives you time to think.

'No thanks.' She watches them trail off down the street, the younger boy swinging an empty bucket, the elder outpacing him, taking the odd puff from a very small cigarette which he holds between first finger and thumb, into his palm. They work their way from door to door. She hears the automatic refusals, the clipped tones, the closing doors. At the end of the road they swing themselves up on to a low wall, the younger boy kicking the heels of his trainers into the bricks, the elder less agitated, staring ahead, to all intents and purposes thinking. Well at least they're not mugging old ladies, she reflects. She walks down the street.

The younger boy sees her coming and instantly jumps down, nudging his companion, who remains impassive.

'How much do you charge?'

'Wassat?'

'I said how much do you charge?'

He begins to blabber: 'We don't charge no more'n a pahnd, do we Briggsy. All we wants is a pahnd. We got a bucket and a cloth and everyfing. All we needs is water. Briggsy an me we never asks no more'n a ...'

'Shaddup.' Briggsy slides off the wall and straightens above her. He flicks some ash from his by now almost invisible cigarette. Finally he speaks: 'Three quid exterior. Five quid exterior and interior combined total clean-up quality job can't say fairer'n that.' Exhausted by his sales pitch he leans back against the wall. His companion looks up at him with admiration and disbelief.

'It seems an awful lot.'

Briggs looks at her as if what she has said either has not been heard, or is beneath his notice.

'It seems a lot.'

'Take it or leave it.'

The space between their eyes is dead. There is nothing in the air that might be touched to sound a lighter note. A Deal has settled over them with the weight of a Mahler symphony. For there is nothing humorous about money. Insurance premiums, mortgage repayments, garage bills may be ludicrous, ridiculous, farcical even but never, in any circumstance, amusing.

'What's your name and where do you live?'

'Whatcha want to know for?' As he rises forward aggressively, Briggs minor instinctively cowers away. Name and address. They was something you never gave away. Ever.

'I don't want it washed at the moment, but when I do I'll need to know where to find you.'

There is a long pause during which the elder boy, staring at a point beyond her, appears to be considering. Finally he says: 'Briggs. Canfield Avenue. Flats.'

'Right. Thanks. I still think five pounds is too much, she adds, and turns away.

'Four-fifty the whole job,' he calls after her. 'Number twenty-six.'

She walks to the Canfield estate. She takes the dog. It is curious how creatures bred to race over turf in pursuit of fur or feather will linger over stained concrete into which countless pools of urine have seeped. It is an effort to pull him up to the second floor. She activates the chimes.

Briggs's mother, or stepmother, or common-law parent, puts her eye to the tiny circle which is her magnifying glass on the hostile world, and opens the door a crack.

'Is Briggsy in? Your son?'

'Which one?'

'The big one. The one who does the car washing.'

'What do you want him for?'

'Can you tell him if he wants to do my car he can come round at the weekend. Sunday would be best. Number nineteen Jessop Street.'

'I'll tell him but I don't know as he'll come.'

'Oh?'

'Working, isn't he. Pizza Parlour.'

'Oh. Right. Thanks anyway.' The door closes quickly on Briggs's unknown life.

The word Parlour, she thinks. Contrasting oddly with the onomatopoeically thin and brittle Pizza. Briggsy pulling corks, taking orders, stretching dough? Somehow she couldn't see it. He was too detached, too centred in himself. Briggsy was an operator, an omphalos. Probably he was also a thinker. She couldn't tell.

He appears the following Sunday with his nervous and excitable assistant and it is as she had feared, one and a half hours of water slopping through the house, borrowed polishes and dusters, vacuum cleaners and extension leads, fractured instructions and expletives, and the horn going off at odd intervals. Briggs minor throws himself into his task with a considerable amount of enthusiasm - she barely prevents him from washing the upholstery - if little finesse. His brother ranges round the car as the small boy works, or sits on the bucket. At the end he opens all the car doors, flicks out (another new) duster and carefully and ostentatiously wipes the seals. Briggs minor's admiration knows no bounds. His brother is a professional, all right.

'Every Sunday?' he says, as he hands back two half-empty mugs.

'No, that's too often. What about every other?'

'Suit yourself. Every week you get a top job.'

She looks at the smeared windows, at the pile of sodden rags and dusters, at the vacuum cleaner and lead tangled up on the pavement and feels that she may not be able to face a top job every week. 'I'll see you the Sunday after next, if that's okay with you.'

'All right then. See ya.'

They come twice more. The first time they are in a hurry - Palace/West Ham three o'clock kick-off - the second she takes out three mugs of tea, both better to oversee the operation and to try to find some route into Briggsy's mind. In neither case is she successful.

'What's your job like?'

'What job?'

'At the Pizza Parlour.'

'He done ever so good to get it. Our mum's ever so pleased and our Danny give him his ...'

Briggsy stops him with a stare.

'All right all right I know. I'm doin it aren't I. I aven't stopped doin it, ave I ..' The boy goes from babbling to silent sloshing under the frown of his elder brother.

'What do you do there?'

'What. Oh, there. Not much.'

'Do you do,' she hesitates, 'restaurant work?'

'Nah.'

'Oh. Well. Do you like it?'

'S'all right.' He turns away. There is no doubt who is in control of this conversation.

'Come on. Hurry up. I aven't got all day.'

She is worried when they fail to turn up for the third appointment, not so much by the fact as by what she imagines might be the reason behind it. He is sensitive, she can see that, and she has been too prying. What, in any case, had been her intention? What would she have done with the information, had he offered any? Briggsy had a right to his own life, the same as anyone else.

She thinks hard before going again to the flat. Finally she summons up the courage. She doesn't take the dog.

Briggsy's mother had made little impression at their first encounter - she had barely caught a glimpse of her - and so this big-boned, violent-eyed woman who suddenly throws open the door and stands before her trembling with sweat and rage, takes her by surprise.

'I ... I was wondering if Briggsy was at home,' she says.

'E's in hospital. Run over.' She slams the door, and from behind it, something between a sob and a scream. 'Probably your fucking pizza.'

He died the following week. It was in the local paper, along with a photograph of the narrow shop-front which was the Pizza Parlour, a fleet of mopeds ranged up outside it, each with its distinctive black box on the back, each with its 'L' plate. Unofficial riders weaving imaginatively through suburban traffic to satisfy casual cravings. Pepperoni Sausage with extra mushroom and garlic. American Hot.

Local outrage: Provisional drivers. Exploitation. Sixteen-year-olds. Children, really... Statements from School: Conscientious student. Brilliant future. Family coming to terms... Statements from the Pizza Parlour: Tragic accident. Training is given. Every effort is made to ensure the safety ...

She didn't go the funeral, 10.30 a.m. 15th September, Church of St. Michael and All Angels, Broad Street, Twickenham. She thought about it, but she didn't go. Yet when evening came, little had been accomplished.

'Hi. You look tired. Bad day? Why don't I send out for a pizza.'

IS ANYBODY LISTENING

Damian didn't know whether he remembered his mother. He remembered photographs of her, because his father used to have some about the place, so perhaps that was what he remembered, the photographs.

There were boys in his class who had parents who were divorced, but most of them lived with their mothers, indeed their mothers seemed desperate to hang on to them and some even went to court to keep them, but his had walked out, walked out and gone to Arizona one day. With an American. When he was two. Just a note on the kitchen table, his father said.

His father said they used to meet in the library, his mother and the American. He, Damian, loved the library because there was an ace pop-up book of Greek myths with Poseidon's trident rising up out of the sea and if you bent the book back along the spine, you could get Poseidon to rise up as well. Damian had spent many afternoons in Children's Books, while his father looked things up. And this was strange, really, because his father didn't much like books that had been written specifically for children. So when he started reading the Greek myths to him he gave him the full, unbowdlerised account, not some watered-down children's version, and he would *be* Jupiter, or Zeus — he always insisted on the Greek names - and hurl thunderbolts (socks, or whatever was to hand) around the room. He was a bit of a show-off, his dad.

His father was a writer. Tom Berringer. He specialised in How To books. How to Improve Your CV, How to Retire at Forty, How to Achieve a Work-Life Balance, although as far as Damian knew he had no particular expertise in any of these matters. He worked at home and hated being interrupted, so Dee had come as a sort of a blessing, Damian supposed, though a mixed one.

They had met her in Regent's Park Zoo, in the reptile house. It was a Saturday afternoon in summer, a really hot one, and his dad had suddenly got fed up and said that zoos smelled, so they had gone into the reptile house and there she was, in little black shorts and an orange top and a lot of space in the middle where they didn't meet. She was with a bunch of kids, three boys, and from the back he thought she was a sister but when she turned round she looked older than sisters ought to look, although her hair was tied up in a pony-tail. She had grabbed his father by the arm and said, 'Oh, you gotta see this! It gives Monty Python a whole noo meaning!' and she and his father had laughed and joked in the reptile house while he and the other kids and their father had stood about feeling embarrassed. She said that whatever it was between herself and his father had been 'instant, chemistry' and wasn't it just the weirdest thing because she had been on a blind date with the *other* father. She had met him through a dating agency because when she filled in the form she had said she didn't mind men with kids. It struck Damian as odd, because she didn't seem very interested in kids, or zoos either, for that matter.

She had come back with them that afternoon and had been in their house more or less ever since. On the Sunday she had collected her stuff from a flat in Earl's Court and dumped it in the spare room and on the Monday she had started her evening classes. She went out nearly every evening during the week, after supper, and Damian was grateful to her for that. It gave him time to be with his dad, and it was the best time of the day.

As soon as she had gone, his father would run around the room singing 'Chick-chick-chick-chick-*chicken*!' doing the elbows, and then they would have another supper, a proper supper, chicken nuggets, or burgers, or bacon and eggs. His dad said it was the only thing he had against her, the vegetarianism, he was fed up with couscous and puy lentils, but Americans have some funny ideas, and anyway she was young, and she did at least cook for them before she went out. Damian was glad to get her out of the house for a bit, because she was very loud, screaming with laughter at her own jokes, or the television, or down the telephone, but he noticed that his father was more cheerful since she had come.

When he prayed, Damon didn't pray that she would disappear or get run over or anything, just that she would go quiet, and stay out of the school playground. He prayed to the gods he knew from his books, the Greek gods, Zeus and Pallas Athene, Apollo and Ares. He always had a quick word with Ares, because there were altogether too many wars going on in the world. He should try to cool it.

On Sundays, his grandad came to lunch. Damian loved his grandad, because his grandad would read to him whatever he wanted for as long as he liked. His grandad was intrigued by Damian's gods. They seemed as real to his grandson as the players in the football team they both supported. Ironic, he thought, when he, his grandad, was forbidden even to mention the word God in the house, an injunction he ignored because Damian loved the bible stories.

'Your father would throw me out if he knew the sort of things we talk about. Come to that, he would probably throw you out too, praying to your gods.'

'It's not really praying.'

'No? What, then?'

'More of a chat, really.'

'How d'you know they're listening?'

'Oh, they're listening all right, but they're very busy. They sometimes take a while to get things done.'

'Why don't you try my God?'

'He's got too much to do, there's only one of him. The thing about my gods is, they're a team, they've each got their own job. It's just a matter of choosing the right one.' The role of grandad's God was very vague, he thought, and probably too much for one person.

All the same, he was feeling somewhat let down by Pallas Athene, goddess of wisdom. He had put her on Dee's case some weeks ago now. Anyone who had sprung, fully-armed, from someone's *brain* ought to be able to sort Dee out, but her behaviour didn't seem to have changed at all. He had asked his father why she was called Dee. His dad said she had been christened Diane but didn't like it and had shortened it to Dee. Well, he was called Damian and didn't like it and there didn't seem to be a thing he could do about it. You can't go around calling someone 'Day.' It was just one of the things that were wrong in his life.

He reckoned it was why he never got any passes in football. That, and the fact that most boys are right-footed and pass naturally to the left. Zak Wilson was at left wing and they sent him nice passes which landed just ahead, so that he could run on to the ball and look really brilliant as he swept down the wing. Whereas it took a while for someone to screw themselves round and shout 'Damian!' and make some sort of pass to the right. The ball always landed just behind him or on his feet so that he had to control it first before attempting that amazing run he knew he was capable of. Sometimes he and his dad practised in the park, but his dad wasn't much good at passing to the right either. One day he was going to get that Zak Wilson in the kind of tackle premier league players get red cards for. He would have to wait until they were put on opposite sides, of course. But if he could do it, it might just lay Zac Wilson up long enough for him, Damian, to take over on the left.

He wished there was a god of football, but in the absence of one he had taken things up with Apollo. He was also negotiating a trip to America with Hermes, the winged messenger. He wanted to visit his mother in Arizona, he wanted to see the desert. His dad had said he could go. At first it was 'when you're six,' then it was 'when you're eight.' Now it was 'when you're ten.' Well, he was nearly ten now and nothing seemed to be happening. He told Dee he would like to visit his mother and to his surprise she said, 'Hey! Why not? Cool!' and went straight in to discuss it with his father. He heard his heavy-voiced reply: 'He doesn't know her. I shouldn't think he even remembers her. She left when he was two.' All the same, he would like to see the desert.

Dee used a lot of little phrases that sounded quite friendly when you first heard them, as if she was warming up to you, but somehow she never did. It was only his Dad she warmed up to. After school she would stand in the kitchen popping popcorn. Sometimes she would wander across with her saucepan and peer over his homework: 'Looks pretty neat to me, Damian, but hey! what do I know?' Or, when he had finished: 'I thought you were supposed to do a half hour of math, but hey! who's counting?' Why did she say *math*, he wondered? No-one else he knew said math, no-one else in the world. It was as if there was only one sum that had to be done, ever. Oh well, perhaps she was really stupid.

The boys at school thought she was nice. Well, not nice exactly, but 'cool' or 'hot', depending on age. Damian really wished she would stay away from school. She would saunter into the playground in her tight shiny jeans and orange fuzzy sweater with the high neck. She had such a way of *walking*, it wasn't normal walking, it was fake, acty walking as if someone had said: 'Now this is how you walk. You put one foot forward and swing your body one way, then you put your other foot forward and swing your body the other way' and she would do that walk right past him, although he could swear she knew where he was, past the mothers stiffening and the fathers watching until she ran into a teacher who would say: 'Ah, Mrs. Berringer. Looking for Damian? I think he's over there by the gate.' And sometimes the teacher would take her by the arm and actually propel her towards him, as if he was planning to introduce them to each other. The times he had begged his father to let him walk home on his own. 'It's only just up the hill. Other boys do it.'

'No, Damian. In our circumstances I like to keep things as normal as possible.' Normal? He wondered why the teachers called her Mrs. Berringer. He supposed they couldn't cope with anything else.

He had decided to dump Pallas Athene. What was needed here was a god, a god with some experience of difficult women. Hephaestus, god of fire, he was the man. He was married to Aphrodite, and she was a handful if ever there was one. He was a top god, Hephaestus, in Damian's book, working at his forge, under the volcano, with his hideous assistants, the giant one-eyed Cyclops, making thunderbolts, lightning, and fire. His father, Zeus, had once chucked him out of heaven, though Damian couldn't remember quite why. He imagined the nine days - *nine days* - in which he hurtled through the air and stars and planets to earth. Really, he was lucky to have got off with only a broken leg.

It was a particularly hot summer evening and Dee was being particularly hot and noisy with the friends who were gathered on the patio of their narrow, stuffy, Kentish Town house. She was shrieking 'Get *outa* here!' where most adults he knew said 'Really?' or 'How interesting' and slapping people on the shoulder. The barbecue had only made things hotter and his dad cross through bending over it and poking it and asking, every now and again, why they couldn't eat inside like normal people. But the friends seemed to be enjoying themselves and Dee was on top form so he had taken his plate and assorted burnt offerings and climbed upstairs to his room at the top of the house where he had a television and a computer and his books. It was a loft extension which had been put on a couple of years ago, as an investment, his dad said. It didn't look anything like the picture the loft conversion company had shown them, and there had been endless rows over the plumbing and the electricity and the people who were supposed to be putting in the sloping windows. His dad said they were all cowboys, it was a botched job, but now that it was finished he liked it, it was his room, although it was very hot in summer.

Tonight it was stifling. The sky, while they were on the patio, had suddenly gone quite dark and looking at it through his windows now he could see that it had turned a livid, purplish colour. He thought he heard rumblings in the distance. He lay back on his bed with his hands clasped under his head.

'Look, Hephaestus', he said. 'Things are not going very well for me down here. I tried that tackle on Zak Wilson today and all that happened was I got a horrible gash on my shins and he was left with the ball and my dad had come to watch and was pissed off with me and went into a long spiel about sportsmanship and dirty play and he-never-thought a-son-of-his. And I've got this weird sort of stand-in mother, only she's not a mother. She's all right, I mean I don't mind her, but she's really loud and she will keep collecting me from school. Can't you do something about that? I mean, you know what she's like, you've seen her. I just want her quietened down a bit and kept out of the school playground. Hey! Are you listening to me? My grandad thinks you don't listen, but I tell him you do. Couldn't you give me a sign, whip up an earthquake or lift the roof off or something? Or just … you know … sort it'.

He ate his supper, sitting cross-legged on the bed. Then he put his plate on the floor and lay back, staring at the tongued-and-grooved pine ceiling. He heard the first, heavy drops of rain.

In the sky, the rumbling grew nearer. And now there was a crack of thunder overhead and the sudden, torrential downpour of rain that sounded as if it was being hurled out of the sky. Across his windows yellow zigzags of lightning streaked and broke, the sky coming to startling electric life. Rain battered the roof. He could feel it shaking. The windows trembled against the wind.

Damian wondered what was going on below. He tried to look down, but the sloping windows showed him only other rooftops. He assumed the barbecue had been washed out. He could still hear voices, though curiously not Dee's. He went to turn on the light. Nothing. He tried the one above his bed. Same thing. There must have been a power cut. And now water was coming through the roof. On to his bed. He moved the bed to one side and pushed a towel under the drip with his foot. He would have to go downstairs and get a bucket. He didn't know whether his father would be pleased or annoyed that he'd been right about the builders.

He made his way carefully downstairs, feeling the wall. They were in the kitchen, the few remaining friends, slumped around the table over glasses and bottles of wine. His father was struggling with a box of matches and Dee's scented tea lights. He had managed to get one going and was putting it on the mantelpiece.

'Ah, here's Damian', he said. 'I must talk to him about tomorrow.'

Tomorrow? What was happening tomorrow? 'I need a bucket', Damian said, 'the roof's leaking.'

'Jesus Christ. That's all I need. Where's the torch.'

He abandoned the tea lights and went to the cupboard under the sink, cursing as he knocked against first the table, then a chair. Kneeling down, he groped about, finally pulling out a large black torch, rubber-clad. The emergency torch, Damian noted. His father pressed the on-off button. He pressed it again, harder, and peered into the bulb. A feeble orange glow flickered and died.

'Oh Jesus bloody Christ. Isn't that just *typical*. Nothing in this house fucking works.'

Damian pulled a cushion off a chair and sat down on the floor.

'Well', his father said, reaching for a bottle and filling up his glass. 'We will just have to wait until someone in this wonderful country sees fit to reconnect us to the twenty-first century. In the meantime my house may very well be a write-off with a tsunami pouring through the roof.'

'It's not that bad, Dad', Damian said. 'It's only a leak.'

'It is bad. Everything's bad. Dee's broken her ankle ...'

'What?'

'Oh she fell over in the rain, bringing in the barbecue stuff.'

'Pissed', a voice said.

'Yes, that too. Anyway she's out of action. Look Damian,' his father crouched down beside him, spilling red wine on to Damian's trousers, 'look. I've been thinking. Do you think tomorrow might be a good day for you to start coming home from school on your own? I mean, I think you're quite sensible. What do you think. We could give it a try?'

'We could give it a try', Damian said. He looked past his father to the window and beyond. The sky still threatened. Rain continued to fall.

'Thanks', he whispered.

INTRODUCING MISS FOUNTAIN

'May I introduce you to Miss Fountain?'

She rises, a little awkwardly, from the piano, a scrambled bar of Schumann interrupted. Tall, the head inclined, the smile eager, the large, bony hand outstretched.

'So pleased.' He touches briefly and withdraws, then turns and makes his way towards the door. He misinterprets. Hers is not the eagerness of lust, or acquisition, but that of innocence, seeking acceptance. She lets the great hand fall and moves, good-humouredly, into another group. The little London soirée gathers her. She has no expectations.

Miss Fountain. A big girl, good-looking, strong in the saddle, riding out before dawn with her father, the crusted winter earth under the hooves, steam rising from the nostrils, from the hot flanks. Her father, the doctor, freed from the tyranny of the invalid's house, throwing his horse over the bare Lincolnshire fields, taking the hedges. A hunt with no fox. And afterwards, the sweet smell of the stables, the red, sweaty hands linking his greased reins with hers:

'Rub them down, girly, and blanket them. I must go and see your sister.'

Her sister's bedroom. The mask, the oxygen tent, the small beads of vapour inside the plastic, the heavy, rasping breathing. The struggle for air, for life. Miss Fountain has friends, now, who are asthmatic. Who reach in their handbags for squat, lipstick-like canisters - hah! - and life goes on. But in their home, their bleak, Fenland farmhouse with the horses kicking and whinnying in the stables and her sister gasping and sweating in her bedroom, the blue eyes closed in pain and fear, the golden curls damp on her forehead ...

'You are very pretty, Miss Fountain.' Her first pupil, emboldened by a Beethoven quartet.

'Oh, but you should see my sister.'

How many times had she almost died? She could not separate them, now. It was easier to drop them into the pool of her recollection and let them swell, like paper flowers, into one image. Her father, pacing the room; their own doctor, called for the umpteenth time; her mother, weeping. In her childhood memory, her mother was always weeping.

'I think we are going to lose her.'

The local hospital at midnight, after the ambulance rush, the crisis which her father and their doctor could not handle. The family waiting, tense, fluorescent-lit, hedging their hope against the specialist's fear. Told to go home, and unable to comply. *'You should get some rest. There's nothing you can do.'* Dawn breaking. Anxious, watery eyes straining to read the specialist's face. *'She's out of danger now. You have been lucky. This time we have pulled her through.'*

Learning her future in the amphitheatre of illness, her mother the music graduate teaching the daughter on her first three-quarter instrument. Hesitant Mozart, beginner's Bach, a simple Corelli adapted by her mother for her young hands. Working at playing as her sister works at breathing. Small, isolated pleasures for her mother. Intervals. And sometimes her father, when patients do not claim him, at the keyboard. An unskilled pianist, but competent. Enthusiastically embracing a role not linked to his profession.

'Your father is worried about your sister's education. She misses so much school. He hopes at least that she may have a life, some sort of occupation. His sister was asthmatic, and her life curtailed. She died at twenty-two.'

Her first full-size viola, bought, not hired. Running her hands over the wood's dark ribbed grain, fingering the strings. Longing for ownership as her parents waver. The obduracy of the vendor, strong in his long years, his expertise. He cannot accept a lower price. He has played it in the London Symphony for thirty years. An instrument like this – Foster, eighteen-hundreds – well, they must know its value. He lets it go with sadness, lowering it into the case one last time, wrapped in an old silk scarf, the chin-rest worn. *'Ambient temperature. No central heating. Care for it as you would a child.'*

Miss Fountain at music school in London, blonde heavy hair and expressive arms, sweeping the bow across the strings of her viola, long fingers making light of the intervals, her body moving with the music. She remembers her father's voice, behind the closed door of the drawing room:

'We must let her go. She has won her place. She must have a life outside her sister's.'

And suddenly, in teenage years, her sister getting better. She, at twenty, in her second year, is told of it:

'You'll be amazed. The tent, the mask, are gone (although we keep them for emergencies). A huge change. Apparently it happens sometimes. Your father is so happy.'

Returning home, a young man on her arm. A scene so different from the one she knew, yet, in a sense, the same. Her father at the piano, her sister on the violin (her hands too small for the darker, richer instrument her father loves) but playing together, her face lovely, effort-free.

'Well, has she talent? Shall we send her to music school, like her sister? She isn't strong. What do you think, young man?'

' I could keep an eye on her. And she has her sister. We will take care of her.'

London. The Royal College. The two sisters together, one now a teacher, one a student. The younger's playing is judged outstanding. She might go far. Recitals are arranged, and competitions, her sister at the piano. But her health is suspect. It would not withstand the rigours of a professional musician's schedule. This is the young man's view. The young man becomes Miss Fountain's sister's lover. And, before long, her husband.

'This is a happy day for you. To see your daughter married, when there were times when you must have thought you'd lost her. And to a doctor, too.'

'Yes, it could not have worked out better.'

'Your eldest is a lovely girl as well. I'm sure she'll marry soon.'

'Oh, I don't know. She no longer brings her young men home. She doesn't let us see them.'

'Where will they live?'

'Near Cambridge. He's joined a practice there.'

'And your eldest?'

'She lives in London. She teaches at the College.'

Miss Fountain takes unpaid leave to help her sister with the birth. It is to be by Caesarian section. It is thought she might not survive a natural delivery. Her husband worries about his frail wife's health, but a lovely baby girl is born. She names the baby Niobe, after her mother. Not that it is her name, but that is how she was. Miss Fountain leaves the little family well. She is delighted with her niece.

'Miss Fountain? A call from your sister's husband.'

'She isn't coping very well with the baby. Could you come up? We'd be so grateful if you would'.

'Is she ill? Is it the asthma again?'

'No. Not the asthma. Please say you'll come.'

Miss Fountain's teaching is being interrupted by her times away. She applies to make her post part-time. Less pay but less commitment, and she feels less guilty for her absences.

'How is your sister?'

'Quite well. Recovering quite well.'

'And the new baby?'

'Bonny. A bouncing boy. They're calling him Daniel, after Barenboim. She hopes for a musician.'

'Your father and I will come at the weekend. If she is well enough.'
'She isn't strong.'
'It's not the asthma again?'
'No. Not the asthma.'

Miss Fountain's niece and nephew, from quite young, are brought to stay. They like their aunt. They find her resolute and cheerful. Their mother often spends whole days in bed. They do not know what's wrong. Their father tells them that she isn't strong.

'I'm leaving him.'
'You can't.'
'I am. I'm serious.'
'Why? It will break his heart. And what about the children?'
'I'm leaving them as well. It will be better for them, in the end. And for him too, perhaps.'
'That isn't true. He worships you. Think of how he's cared for you, through the years.'
'That's half the trouble. I want to live.'
'Where will you go? You shouldn't be alone.'
'He's taking me to London.'
'He?'
'You surely didn't think I'd go off on my own.'
'Who is he?'
'He runs an antique shop in the village. It's been going on for months.'
'Married?'
'Yes. But he has a flat in London. That's where we'll go. Can you come up and hold the fort?'

The house is sad, the children lost and angry. Grief without death. Miss Fountain is ill at ease with her sister's husband. She senses he sees her as complicit in a plot. Her mother feels the same.

'How could you let her do it? You must have known.'

'Not until just before she went.'
'Why didn't you talk some sense into her?'
'I couldn't have stopped her. No-one could. She just - ran off.'
'That poor man. How will he cope? And the children ...'
'I don't know.'
'Stay with them for a while.'
'I intend to. But I can't be here forever.'

Miss Fountain's career has picked up in recent years. She rarely touches the viola now, but her piano playing is skilled and she is in demand as an accompanist, and for recitals. She has a wide repertoire, without affectation. Scott Joplin comes as easily to her as Beethoven. Her large hands make light of Gershwin. *Rhapsody in Blue* she plays with passion.

'You know that he's married again?'
'It's no surprise. They are divorced.'
'I think your sister might have let us know. Or you.'
'I didn't know myself until the children phoned. It was a quiet wedding. They like her very much.'

Miss Fountain hears infrequently from her sister. She and the lover (they have not married) have moved to Brighton, taking the lease on an antique shop in the Lanes. She rarely sees the children. She is not well, despite sea air. She is bored, and enervated. She has no interest in the *objets de vertu* that they sell. She feels that, on the whole, her sister has had the happier life.

'To Florence? How long for?'
'The summer. It's a Summer School. Run by the British Council.'
'Who will you teach?'
'Students. Musicians who start their training in the Autumn and want to spend the summer months improving their technique, or playing chamber music.'

'That will be nice for you. You may find you have a pupil with great talent. Someone like your sister.'

'Miss Fountain.' The small, dark man touches her shoulder. 'You won't remember me. I taught Voice at the College when you were a student. I am at the *Conservatoire* here in Florence now. I remember your name, because it was like your playing. Didn't you have a sister?'

Miss Fountain hesitates. Voices in the room buzz round her. She lifts her eyes to the flaking, frescoed walls. Flat profiles of the early *quattrocento* withhold condemnation.

'I had. But she died.'

'How sad.' He steers her towards the piano. 'They would like to hear me sing. Will you accompany? What shall we give them? A little Mahler, do you think? Or Wolf?'

Miss Fountain glances round the room, appraising the company. 'Schumann, perhaps?'

'How wise.'

He claps his hands. 'Ladies and gentlemen. Please take your seats. This evening we would like to offer you a little Schumann. But first...' he takes her hand, leads her forward, 'may I introduce to you... Miss Fountain.'

LONDON PRIDE

'Forgive the mess. The garden was my wife's domain.'

He walked ahead of her up the path. Forget-me-nots, grown long and rangey, brushed against her legs. Thin stems of heuchera lay on their sides, defeated. Wind and rain had battered the borders into ragged submission. Only London Pride stood smartly to attention, its delicate pink flowers holding up bravely, the stems secure in their fleshy green boles. 'I love London Pride,' she said automatically, bending down to brush her hand over the heads.

'Grows like a damn weed. Dug the whole thing over twice, but it keeps coming back. Can't think what anyone sees in it, great mass of leaf and puny little flower.'

'I suppose it's because it's old-fashioned,' she said. 'It reminds me of my childhood.'

'That's what my wife used to say.'

The door was ajar and she followed him in. It was a sunny, well-proportioned house, a small Georgian rectory. She wished she could bring herself to want it. Its owner hovered before her uncertainly, heavy brows lowered, avoiding her gaze. A cravat, tied too tight inside an open-necked shirt revealed a veined, white neck at odds with the tanned, lined face above it. An old fawn cardigan clung feebly to its few remaining buttons.

'Look,' he said abruptly, addressing some point beyond her. 'I'm going to get myself some breakfast. Wander round, take measurements or whatever it is you do. Call me when you've finished.' He walked through into the kitchen and she heard him moving crockery around. He had a brief conversation with what was probably a dog. She walked into the study.

Photographs in silver frames covered every surface. She bent to pick one up. As she did so he came into the room, a piece of toast in one hand. She started up guiltily, as if surprised in some act of theft. He took a bite of the toast. Crumbs gathered in the folds around the corners of his mouth.

'This is all a mistake,' he said. 'I'm not selling. You'd better go.'

She stared at him, uncomprehending. 'Is something the matter?'

'Yes. You are. Please leave. Now.'

A wave of rage swept over her. She felt her face redden. 'With pleasure. And may I say you are without doubt the rudest man I have ever met.'

'Quite possibly. It can't be helped.' He ushered her outside and shut the door firmly behind her. Tears sprang to her eyes. Angrily, she blinked them away. The *For Sale* notice wobbled as she pulled the gate sharply behind her.

'Well, that was a waste of time.'

'Mum, I'm sorry.' Her son's voice on the telephone sounded uncharacteristically contrite.

'David. I don't want to live in the country. I don't know what I want, but I don't want that. I'm happy in London, as happy as I'm likely to be.'

'But you can't go on living in that big old house on your own. It's ridiculous, on four floors.'

'I managed all right when your father was alive. I can still ...'

'You need to look ahead, Mum. At least think about a flat. Let me look for one for you and a buyer for the house. I won't put it on the market, I'll just pass the word around. You're lucky to have me in the business, you know.'

David would concentrate his efforts on finding her a flat. She would look at them, of course. It might even be quite fun. After all, she was not obliged to buy. She would always be able to find some sticking-point, some perfectly valid reason why they were unsuitable. She felt sure of it.

What she had not anticipated was a buyer. For her house. The telephone call came some months later when she was sitting in the garden. She picked up the mobile David had given her for Christmas.

The caller's husband was to be posted to London in a year's time. There was therefore no rush. But she had been in touch with David's agency and he had suggested they take a look at number 32 Well Street whilst they were in London this weekend. She used words like early stages, pre-contractual and vendor. She was calling from Ghent.

Joanna was outraged. She agreed to let them see the house on Saturday.

The windows badly needed cleaning, and she was glad. Glad, too, that she had not had the hall repainted nor the worn stair carpet replaced. She left the breakfast things on the table and the washing up in the sink. The cat's food smelled nastily in a bowl on the floor. She opened another can and left it on the worktop with the lid off.

The couple were young and charming and they loved her house. With two young children, it would be ideal. The wife had lived nearby when she was a child, and knew the area. The husband, an American banker, was evidently a man used to making swift decisions. The house had charm. He would look no further. He would telephone the agent first thing Monday.

Somehow she could not bring herself to tell her son that she didn't want the charming couple to have her house. That she couldn't bear to leave it, that the thought of it was making her feel ... unsteady.

'Suppose I can't find anywhere I like?'

'Mum. You don't have to. You can rent. You can rent until you find a place. With the sort of money he's willing to pay, you can probably rent for the rest of your life.'

'But I don't want to. I can't face all that upheaval twice. I'm not sure that I can face it once. David ...'

He cut her short. 'Mum. You're going wobbly. This is a terrific deal. You'd be a fool not to take it.' He was beginning to lose patience with her. She detected the bullying tone, the shift in language.

'I'm sure you're right.' She put the phone down quickly. She would speak to him again later. In the meantime she wandered round the house, her house, still her house, touching curtains and tables and walls. She remembered a poem she used to like, Old House. A line *It was bought with all our earned money* made her cry, and she sat down on the sofa and held her head in her hands. Yes, he was right. She was probably going wobbly. If only she were different, stronger, less ... provisional. If only she could see a future that was not rooted in her past.

In the event, it was David who phoned her. The sale was going ahead. He trusted she had got over her jitters. He was calling because Mrs. Wagner's father wanted to view the house.

'Who is Mrs. Wagner?'

'Come on, Mum. Get a grip. Mr. and Mrs. Wagner are buying your house.'

So final. She panicked. 'The contract hasn't been drawn up yet?'

'Not yet. But Mrs. Wagner's father has been asked to take some measurements. He's quite old, about your age, so you'll probably have to give him a hand. He's coming up from the country some time next week.'

She recognised immediately the figure who stood in the doorway, the lined, tanned face, the heavy eyebrows which she remembered as lowered and threatening. She stepped back involuntarily.

He smiled and held out his hand. 'Mrs. Anderson. I apologise for calling unannounced. I had your telephone number but I'm afraid I lost it. If this is an inconvenient moment I will come back some other time.'

He looked at her questioningly, and she searched for some sign of recognition. There was none.

'Forgive me. I haven't introduced myself. My name is Michenor, Edward Michenor. I am the father of Susan Wagner, whose husband is buying your house.'

He had brought a builder's tape but was evidently unused to its caprices, cursing and dropping it as it snapped back on to his hand. She watched him from the kitchen, an amused smile spreading across her face.

'You haven't got an ordinary tape measure, have you? This bloody thing's going to have my fingers off.'

'It would be all right if I held one end. Here, let me help you.'

She fetched the ladder and they spent two hours measuring windows, alcoves, stair widths, ceiling heights. She saw that ascending the ladder made him breathless, so that she stayed him with her hand:

'Here, let me. I'm used to it.' She stepped up nimbly and he handed her the tape.

'Goodness, you're in good nick.'

'It's the three flights of stairs. My son thinks I should join a gym and lift weights and do workouts. This house is my workout.'

'Oh, children', he said. 'They always think you should be doing something other than what you are. It's role reversal. I see it as revenge for all those hours of homework and having to go to bed on summer evenings when it was still light.'

Her blue eyes smiled down at him. 'So. Would you do things differently, armed with the wisdom of age?'

'I wouldn't call it wisdom. Experience, perhaps. And no, I don't suppose I would. As parents, we just do the best we can, don't you think?' He took her hand as she stepped down from the ladder.

She made some tea and they sat at the kitchen table whilst he took a fair copy of the measurements, and she spiked the originals. New curtains would certainly perk up the drawing room. She would go and look at fabrics on Friday.

'It's a lovely house.'

'Yes.'

'How long have you lived here?'

'Practically all our married lives. It was our first house.'

'And your husband?'

'He died two years ago. I still haven't quite ...I'm still not ...'

'Not sure that you want your world *bouleversé* ? Again?'

'Yes, that's it. That's it exactly. I can't see the way clear, you understand. I can't ...' She brushed her hair from her face and he saw the darkness in her eyes. She rose and moved towards the ladder.

'Here. Let me take that for you. Where does it live?'

'Outside. It hangs on the wall.'

She followed him out. 'Thank you. You don't want to measure the garden then?'

He caught her humour and his eyes responded. 'I don't think so. It's not on my instruction sheet. It's pretty,' he said, looking beyond her. 'Not that I know much about it. My wife was the gardener.'

'I know.'

He looked at her quickly. She walked down the steps and he followed her. Deceived by a late summer sun, pale tobacco plants gave out their heady evening scent. A few perennials struggled on.

'London Pride,' he said, bending to touch it. 'Grows like a damn...' He straightened suddenly and stood facing her. 'Oh my God,' he said. 'Oh God. I thought I had seen you somewhere, sometime. Oh God. I was terribly rude to you. You came to see my house. I was unforgivably rude.'

'You were.'

'How awful. How awful that I shouldn't have remembered. I'm sure you remember every word.'

'I do.'

'How awful. I should have telephoned you to apologise. The thing was, my wife ... my wife had died after a long illness. I was at a loss.'

He paused, distracted. She sat down on the garden seat, and he leaned against the arm. 'Susie was in Ghent with Philip and the kids and she got it into her head that I shouldn't be left in the rectory on my own. I can't think why. I'm not gaga you know, Joanna.'

She turned towards him, startled.

'Your name was on an envelope on the kitchen table. Do you mind?'

'Of course not.' Joanna. Something flickered in her that had been long dead. Was it the way he said it, or simply the shock of hearing it, her name, after so long, like that?

'She wanted me to move. Where to, I don't know. We used to live in this area you know, when she was little.'

'I know.'

'I liked it. I used to really like it. There were nice restaurants around.'

'There still are.'

'Anyway, I rebelled. I dug my heels in and rebelled. You were the first person to see my house, and the last. I'm afraid you got the brunt of my rebellion. And my rudeness.'

'Well, you did the right thing. The rebellion, I mean.' She rose and he followed her back towards the house. The afternoon sun caught the faded lights of her hair, once auburn. She had been a pretty woman, too thin for the fashion of her age.

'I would like ...... I would really like ...... I mean if you would allow me......something, you know ..... something to make up .....'

'You have.'

He looked at her.

'I love this house. I love it and I'm happy here. I don't want to move. Why should I? I'm digging my heels in. I'm not going.'

He put a hand on her shoulder. 'I'm glad.'

'But your daughter and her family?'

'They'll find somewhere else. This is your house. You belong here. Charming old house, charming ...'

'Old lady?'

'Owner, I was going to say.'

'I shall have to tell my son. He won't understand. He has a heart of gold, but he won't understand.'

'People with hearts of gold often have iron fists.'

She raised her eyebrows.

'They like to keep you in situations determined by themselves. It frees up their own lives. Tyranny must be resisted, you know, even from our children. Especially from our children.'

It's going to be hard,' she sighed.

They walked through the house and into the hall, dim now in the evening light.

'Not as hard as leaving your home. Believe me.' He took the telephone from its cradle and moved a chair towards her. 'Now,' he said, 'you telephone your son. I'm not leaving until you do.'

STRAWBERRY FIELDS

'Hey!'

'Hey!'

'How's it going?'

'Good. It's goin' good.'

'You got some business today?'

'I gotta couple want to go out to the islands. Want a day trip to the islands.'

'Locals?'

'Don't reckon so. Looked like they was visitors. I better get that engine fixed. I shoulda got it fixed before.' The boy knelt down in the boat and pulled the starter cord. The engine sputtered feebly into life, and died. He stood up, splaying his feet against the swaying of the boat. He was frail, slim and shadowy in the dim light of the boathouse, thin-limbed, dark-skinned, long black hair caught in a rubber band at the nape of his neck. 'Yup. I shoulda got it fixed before.'

'You want to, you can take my boat. I gotta get the Ute. I gotta take the wife upstate. She still crazy for buyin' a plot upstate. She still dreamin' strawberry farms.'

'What she say about the island?'

'She don't know yet.'

'Reckon you're gonna be real busy.'

'Which is why I need to humour her a bit. Which is why I need to drive her upstate today.'

'Okay. Thanks, Karl.'

'Sure.' The heavy, fair-haired German punched the boy's shoulder affectionately. 'You have a good day, now. You give them a good day out.'

The boy watched as his friend stepped out of the boatshed and on to the quay. He watched him as he made his way back up the hill, blue jeans low on thick hips, checked trucker's shirt aged with oil and sweat. He'd been good to him, this second generation Canadian, with his uncertain boat-hire business and his Ute and his young Japanese wife with her dreams of upstate plots and strawberry fields.

The two boats rocked against each other in the boatshed, the water slapping in the turbulence of early-morning activity. The boy checked his watch. Six-thirty. It could take an hour to fix his engine. More, perhaps, since he didn't know what was wrong. He'd take Karl's boat. Give him time for coffee and a sandwich before he picked up the old couple at the pier.

They were waiting for him when he ran the boat alongside and tied up, a couple in their sixties, dressed against any eventuality of weather. The wife, small, thin-featured, looked cold, despite a grey anorak zipped to the neck, and the sun, which had already dispelled the dawn chill. The husband, taller but less upright, carried a high colour across his sunken cheeks. He moved with difficulty, his breathing laboured. In one hand he held a rucksack which he swung down into the boat. The boy took it and stowed it under a seat. Then he put one foot up on the pier and holding the boat steady with the other, held out a hand to the wife.

'Easy does it. I got you. I reckon we're going to get a good day. I reckon sun's goin' to come out good.'

'I hope so.'

He helped the husband down, pulled the wet rope in after him and pushed away from the jetty with his hand. Turning into the Sound he started up the engine. The boat moved easily through the water, leaving a wake of low ripples. He took the tiller and settled himself comfortably against the stern sheets. Behind him the Vancouver shoreline dissolved into the mountains. The wife screwed up her eyes against the glare:

'So beautiful. So long since we were here.'

'Vancouver? Lovely. Why now?'

'Oh, I haven't seen Cliff in a while. There are things we need to discuss. Business things. We'll stay with them a week or so. Give you a chance to catch up with Annie and the kids.'

'We'll take a trip to the island?'

'I don't know. It may not be so easy, staying with them. Plus we don't have a boat any more.'

'We can hire one.'

'All of us? Cliff and Annie and all?'

'No. Just the two of us. Sentimental journey. I couldn't bear to be there and not to see it.'

He smiled and touched her hair. 'I know,' he said.

She looked out over the boy's head and tried to keep a fixed point in her sights. She had never meant to stay in this country, had planned to travel the world - America, Australia, the Far East. She remembered their first visit to the island, Ethan, his brother Clifford and herself, one humid, overcast summer's day. The unexpected nostalgia, the cutting back in time, as they jumped out of the boat and waded towards the shore, dragging the boat behind them, the bottom rasping against the stones. The ice-cold water filled her canvas pumps and chilled her legs.

'Like home', she had said.

Ethan had looked up sharply. 'Tell me,' he said.

They picked their way across the stones. 'These islands.'

'Yes?'

'It's what I know. Small, Scottish islands where you're never not aware of the sea and the weather. All the young ones leave, of course. As I did.'

'You want to go back?'

'I'm not saying that. My country is old and inward-looking but I understand it. Your country is new and fluid and I don't yet know what to make of it.'

'What would it take to make you stay?'

'Oh, an island, of course', she had laughed. This one will do.'

'Where you folks from?'

She roused herself, startled. Her husband was asleep, head down and bobbing with the rhythm of the engine.

'Alberta. Kneehill County, north of Calgary.'

'Farmers?'

'No. We used to farm. Now we import farm machinery. From Denmark. We hire it out on contract.'

'What's so good about Danish? Ain't there no Canadian farm machinery?'

She looked at the young man. He was probably about seventeen but looked younger in his shorts and faded polo shirt.

'I expect there is. But Danish machinery is good. And there are a lot of Danes in Alberta.'

'Okay.'

'Is this your business?'

'Nope. It's Karl Reissen's business. He lets me keep a boat there summer time. Winter time I take it out of the water and keep it up the coast at my folks place.'

'Are you in college?'

'Nope. Indians don't go to college too much.'

'Why not?'

'Just don't seem to.'

'What will you do?'

'Same as we've always done. Us West Coast Indians have always lived off the sea.'

'Nice life, if you can make ends meet.'

'I don't need much,' he said.

Ethan watched his wife from under half-closed lids. Above the engine, and the churning water, he caught snatches of conversation. Why did she still talk about the farm, when it had been divided up and sold off years ago? He regretted it, along with subsequent business ventures. The farm machinery business had only recently begun to look up. His Danish mother had nephews in the State who had managed to persuade the local farmers against the machinery they were used to. He had had to cut the nephews in, of course, but it would be worth the price.

They were headed up into Georgia Strait now, a string of islands to the west, the Pacific Ranges and broken British Columbian coastline to the east. The sweet smell of summer sea filled his nostrils. Beside the boat a loon, a black-throated diver, raised its neck and disappeared under the water. He didn't feel secure, even now. How much did a man need to feel secure?

The boy turned the boat west, away from the mountains. He liked these runs between the islands. They called for skill and knowledge. He throttled the engine back and took it carefully, letting the boat absorb the wash from the rocks, holding a course where the current ran deep. He knew these waters, they were in his blood, from the time when, as a small boy, he had first sailed out of Howe Sound with his father and his father had taken his hand and placed it, with his own, on the tiller, so that he should learn, as if by instinct, the strange, dangerous interchange between man and sea. His father had skills and equipment no longer used or lawful: traps, nets, hooks and spears, a toggling harpoon for hunting whales, knives for stripping the pelts of sea otters. His father was a Haida Indian. He reckoned the coast and islands belonged to them.

She would have married him anyway, but shortly after that first visit Ethan and Clifford had taken out a loan and bought Nassett Island. She had looked on it as a sort of wedding present. Their backer was a developer, waiting on a change in planning laws which Clifford said would never happen. For many years the two brothers and their families had summered on the island. They were not allowed to build, not even a log cabin, but they camped, or slept under the sky, and their children learnt to love wild places.

The old man watched the younger as he negotiated the groups of islets and rocky stacks which guarded Nasset at its southernmost point. He had cut the speed right back, the engine a notch above idling, forward propulsion scarcely detectable as the boat rose and fell on the rising waves and vigorous currents between the rocks. Black-backed and herring gulls had colonised these southern outcrops, rising and screaming off their nests as the boat approached. On the stacks, guillemots stood, thick and black against the rock, the stone below white with their guano. Its foul stench reached them as they rounded the point.

The island came suddenly into view, as it always did, as if the string of small islands and stacks had been dropped into the sea, an afterthought, to screen it. Just under a mile long, and half a mile across at its widest point, it lay low on the water, its rough coast rising to a hog's back of grass and sea pinks and brambles and stunted shrubs. She remembered when the children had found wild strawberries and run with them to the beach.

'You'd never sell, Ethan, would you. Not even if Clifford wanted to?'

'Trust me,' he'd said.

The children had tipped the berries out at their feet, tiny piles of jewels among the stones, their faces flushed, their hands and pockets stained.

The boy cut the engine and hauled it out of the water. He jumped out and pulled the boat sideways up the beach, setting up a narrow, barred plank, down which he helped the couple to the shore.

'This where you wanted? Guess it's all right to land.'

'Yes. This is it.'

'I was thinkin' I might go up coast a bit. Do some fishin'. Pick you up later. All right with you?'

'Fine,' Ethan said. 'Come back around four. In time to get us back for supper.'

She felt the stones under her feet and knelt to pick one up, small, smooth, warmed by the sun. She slipped it into her pocket. Something very close to happiness crept over her. The business was doing well, now. Both their sons were partners. Ethan could afford to relax a little, to step aside, to take time to visit this place she loved and which they had seen so little in recent years. One day there would be grandchildren. She would bring them here.

She turned to Ethan and took his hand and together they walked up the path to the place where the children had found strawberries. 'Let's have our picnic here,' she said.

At four they stood where he had set them down. At five he had not arrived. At five-thirty the woman began to hope that he would not arrive, that they might be left there, thrown back on themselves like in the old days. She knew the thought was foolish. They had no food, no extra clothing or protection. Her husband's beta blockers and angina pills were back in her sister-in-law's bathroom, neatly laid out. Anxiety replaced fatalism. At last the sound of an outboard reached them and the boat approached and slowed up before them, its skipper betraying no sense of urgency. He helped them in and pushed off from the shore with an oar, then put both oars in the rowlocks and rowed a little, taking pleasure in the action, in the sound of the blades dipping and drawing the water.

'What kept you?'

'Nothin'. Was I late? Just went upshore a little ways further than I thought. Forgot about the time.'

'Well, we were glad to see your boat.'

'She ain't my boat,' he said. He pulled in the oars and started up the engine, his eyes on the passage ahead.

The sun had lost its warmth and a stiff breeze had blown up and the boy saw that white foam was licking round the rocks.

'You folks always come out to Nassett?'

'Oh yes. We've been coming here for years. We spent our honeymooon here. Under canvas.' She laughed. 'It was a long time ago.'

'Yeah. Pity they're going to build. Spoil it.'

'Build?'

'Yeah. Island's been sold. My partner, Karl, he's gonna make some business from it. Gonna be runnin' the buildin' materials. They got permission for twelve cabins, seven to the southside, five to the north.'

The woman gripped the wood beneath her. 'When did this happen? When? When?'

'Coupla days ago. Two gentlemen come down the waterfront with a real estate agent. Karl picks 'em up, takes them out to the island in his boat and they come back and sign the deal in a bar. Same day.'

He turned the boat towards open water and gave the engine full throttle. The cries of the herring gulls were lost in its clamour.

MRS. GRAEBNER'S SPECIAL INTRUCTIONS

The way she sashays down street, head in the air, hips going. Brushing past me into the house where she shares a flat and where I now live alone. With never a backward glance at me. And after all we've been through.

I can't say I'd ever liked her. Admired her, yes - you have to acknowledge style when you see it. But she always looked to me like a creature you couldn't get close to. Unless you were Mrs. Graebner.

Mrs. Graebner owns the best part of the large Belsize Park house where I have bought a flat. She occupies the top floor where she has a roof garden and pots of geraniums some of which get blown off in high winds and crash into smithereens on my paved patio. When, in the summer, I work outside, I move the table close to the house. A garden flat can be air strike territory. My rooms are large and airy and as minimalist as an untidy newspaper journalist can make them. The bedroom and living room give on to the garden. Being half underground, in the manner of Victorian terraced houses, it is cool in summer and cold in winter. I shall probably sell and move on in a year or so. Back to Mrs. Graebner? Possibly. I know she would love to get her hands on it again. Mr. Graebner deeply regretted selling it, apparently. 'But we needed capital, Mr. Harris. Mr. Graebner, he was very ill. Needed operation very quick, very much money for private treatment. Alas, it was no good. But he died in a beautiful hospital.'

Mr. Graebner had been in the theatre. Or that was how Mrs. Graebner liked to put it. In fact he had been in theatrical props. I think he ran a company that rented them out. He had a warehouse in Streatham and specialised in what he called Russian Interiors. 'Chekhov, Ibsen, Strindberg, Mr. Harris' - Mrs. Graebner had a rather wide-ranging view of Russian literature - 'any time you are seeing a West End play by one of these great writers, you are looking at Mr. Graebner's furniture.'

Which probably accounts for the very peculiar *ambience* of Mrs. Graebner's flat. Despite being high up, it is very dark. Lampshades in orange and parchment yellow, deeply fringed, cover every bulb, so that the light would seem to come not so much from electricity as pumpkins . Heavy furniture and screens fill the floor space, and every surface is covered with yellowing lace runners, hardly visible beneath an astonishing array of once colourful painted clockwork toys. Occasionally one of these may catch you unawares, like the monkey drummer in his faded bell-boy hat which, unannounced and apparently unprovoked, starts beating a little tin drum with rigid ferocity. 'Is the mechanism,' Mrs. Graebner explains. 'Faulty, my dear. Mr. Graebner, he was always going to mend.' I used to wonder if it did it in the middle of the night, when she was trying to get to sleep, in fact whether, all through the night and all over her flat, things sprang violently and randomly to life. Well perhaps they do and perhaps they don't and perhaps she doesn't mind. She still misses Mr. Graebner a lot. He died last year and that was when Samantha came.

She had attitude, even then, never pausing to acknowledge the other residents, despite a great deal of interest from Mrs. Graebner's several tenants. 'You're much too good to her, Mrs. Graebner,' I said one day. 'She takes you for granted. I wouldn't give her house room myself.'

'Mr. Harris, you are very naughty,' she said, her eyes twinkling. 'You know I love that cat. And I think you do too,' she added provocatively. 'Is sweet. Is only a kitten.' Kitten? I don't think Samantha was ever a kitten. Sleek, brown, with a touch of Egyptian about her, I think she sprang, fully formed, from the flank of some warrior race of cats, some ancient breed that had survived through skulduggery and stealth. How else to account for those sudden leaps, when she would arrive out of nowhere to settle, like a snowflake, on my pile of papers. She slept not, like an ordinary cat, curled up, but with paws held out in front of her and head erect, a heraldic cat, a cat *couchant*. Was she asleep? Was she ever asleep? I would look at those outstretched paws, at the coiled musculature of her hindquarters, tensed to spring. The pose disturbed me. Sometimes I put aside my work and bent down close, trying to catch her out. But she held fast. Only when I had taken up my work again would she roll over and give her underbelly to the sun. 'There you are,' the gesture seemed to say, 'just a normal cat.'

'*Mister* Harris.' Mrs. Graebner rings on my bell one evening last February. Her old face is heavy with make-up, her dyed red hair caught behind her ears with two pink butterfly clips. 'So sorry for disturbing you. I am for hospital next week. My operation. Finally they send for me. You will look after Sammy while I am away?'

No thought of a refusal. No grovelling request. 'Oh, I'm not sure about that, Mrs. Graebner. I'm out all day. I'm not sure I could ... anyway I may have to go away. Abroad. Assignments.'

'Nonsense, Mr. Harris. You are never away. Tomorrow you come to me for special instructions. I show you where I keep her food. One half tin each day. With milk if you have it. It doesn't matter.'

'I'm not having her *here*.'

'There is no need. I have a cat flap in my door. She comes and goes as she pleases. But you may have her with you, if you wish. As long as she is let out during the day. Is as it pleases you, Mr. Harris.'

It doesn't please me. It doesn't please me at all. How dare she assume? I screw up the paper I have been working on and throw it angrily across the room. Bloody cat.

Mrs. Graebner is to be away for ten days, possibly two weeks. The first day I forget all about Samantha. The editor has pulled the next day's cover story and we all stay late. Several beers have passed under the bridge before I make it home and throw myself on to the bed, exhausted. A persistent scraping sound keeps me from sleep.

Outside on the patio Mrs. Graebner's cat is running her claws down my French windows. On the glass, mark you, not the wood, though to be fair to her there is precious little wood. It sets my teeth on edge. 'Okay, okay. I'm sorry, I forgot. I'm coming.' I run up the stairs, twisting my ankle in my haste, and let myself into Mrs. Graebner's pumpkin flat. It is a curious place at the best of times. Without her in it, it gives me the creeps. The tins of cat food are lined up in her kitchen, a rusty Scout's can opener at the ready. 'This is disgusting,' I say, as the tin gives up its unmistakable smell. Dangerous, too. I contemplate the frilled, uneven circle that was the lid, hanging by a thread of metal to its container. 'Look,' I tell my charge, who seems suddenly enormous and is rearing, cat *rampant*, at my feet, 'number one, I have an electric can opener. Number two' (feeling my swollen foot), 'I am not coming up here every night. In future, you will dine downstairs.'

But no amount of persuasion, the following evening, will entice her to my flat. I hold the half-empty tin, I walk backwards down the stairs saying, 'Puss, puss, puss, come on puss, nice Kitekat, puss. Come along puss, come to Jonathan's nice flat.'

'The cat is called Samantha.' One of Mrs. Graebner's English-speaking tenants passes me on the stairs. 'Sammy. She answers to her name.'

'Thank you. I know.' Maybe it's the tin. I scoop the food into her bowl and repeat the process. No dice. Cat sits in Mrs. Graebner's doorway unmoving. Cat *sejant*.

'Okay, you win. But *tomorrow* you dine downstairs.'

Saturday finds me in the ironmonger's purchasing - I can hardly believe myself - a cat flap.

'What size, sir?'

Size? Size? A cat is a cat, isn't it?

Several cat flaps, bubble-wrapped so that it is impossible to inspect the mechanism, are produced. They look complicated, though more or less the same size.

'What's the difference?'

'Very little, actually. But if your cat is not a very large one, I would advise the smallest. It keeps out the larger neighbourhood cats. And of course small dogs.'

Small dogs? That's all I need.

'Isn't there a type that lets in only your own cat?'

'Sir. The person who invented that would be a millionaire.'

The evening finds me with Ralph, my mate from the news desk, sawing a hole in the garden door of my living room. The cat flap instructions have defeated me. Ralph has taken over.

'You're mad,' he says. 'It isn't even your cat.'

'I know. But I'm not going to let it beat me. If its tiny little brain says: Cat flap - food, then that's what's going to happen. Down here. I refuse to go up to Mrs. Graebner's every night.'

'On the other hand,' Ralph has not been listening, 'it could be a selling point when you come to move. A lot of single people have cats.'

Sunday the cat doesn't get fed at all. In fact, I don't see it. It hasn't come in through my new, inviting flap and it isn't upstairs either. Perhaps it's dining out, I think, without conviction. This is a most ungrateful animal. Really, it doesn't deserve to live in one of the gastronomic capitals of the world.

On Monday I visit Mrs. Graebner in hospital. She is practising walking, with the aid of a physiotherapist, down the hospital ward, a man's red dressing grown wrapped around several layers of nylon nightdress, fluffy pink slippers on her feet. She has her make-up on, and five pink rollers in her theatrical red hair.

'Mr. Harris! Come here and give me your arm. I am doing very well, as you see. I am the model patient.'

I lead her back to her bed where she takes out her rollers, carefully placing them in a fold of the *Daily Mail*, open on her bed. 'There. Ready for receiving royalty,' she laughs. 'And now tell me. How is my little Samantha? How are you two getting along?'

'Oh fine. Fine.'

'You are becoming great friends, I can see it. Is she eating? I hope she is not pining for me?'

'Oh no. She's eating fine.'

'What did she eat last night, Mr. Harris? What nice little tin did you open for her last night?'

'What do you mean? I thought they were all the same.'

'Mr. Harris! You have not noticed? Of course, you are teasing me. There is rabbit, tuna, salmon, chicken - the chicken is her favourite, don't you agree?'

'Oh yes.'

'So what did she have last night? Give me the picture.'

'The chicken. Yes, she had chicken last night.'

'I am so glad. Chicken on Sunday, that is very suitable. Thank you, Mr. Harris. You are a good man.'

On Wednesday it snows. I haven't seen the cat for four days. No-one in the house has seen her since - they can't quite remember - the weekend, they think. I am now really worried. Worried - and angry. This cat is not my responsibility. I'm simply feeding her. How am I supposed to know what she gets up to? She isn't living with me. Then I remember the cat flap. Could I be sued? Mrs. Graebner spends a lot of time at the Citizen's Advice Bureau. Perhaps I could be sued.

I put on my wellingtons and trudge out into the street, calling her name, softly at first, then louder as anxiety overtakes embarrassment. 'Samantha! Sam! Sammy!' If she wouldn't come to me for food, it's unlikely that my voice will entice her now. 'Damn her!' I say at the door, stamping the snow from my boots.

'That's right, mate. Women, they're not worth it.'

In the unlikely event that Samantha may come through the flap, I decide to sleep in the sitting room, though 'sleep' is an inexact description of my night's activity. After midnight it begins to snow again, large flakes falling thickly. I have not drawn the curtains. I put on my overcoat and open the door on to the patio. A blast of cold air hits me and snow flies up into my face. There is a torch in my pocket. I shine it outside.

There is nothing quite as spellbinding as falling snow. Whether it's that you can see but not hear it, or that the mundane is being transfigured before your eyes, everyday outlines blurred and purified.

I pull the door closed and turn to go into the kitchen. On the pale carpet, stretched out at my feet, is the cat. She is wet, her fur matted and black-looking, apart from a deep gash that runs from below her eye down to and past her shoulder. The skin has been torn away, and on bending down I see that so has her foreleg. It is attached to her body by the slenderest of muscle fibres.

'Oh God. Oh cat. What has happened to you? Oh my God.' She has not flinched as I kneel to look at her. Her eyes are nearly closed.

'Don't die. Please don't die. Oh my God.' Keep her warm. Mustn't touch the wound. Making a sort of cage over her body from the fire guard, I put my coat over it. I rush upstairs to Mrs. Graebner's flat for the vet's number. Shaking, I punch in the digits. An Answerphone message directs me to the emergency veterinary service. Bloody hell. Why does everything happen in the middle of the night? She'll die if I don't get her to someone. But I can't move her, I don't know how to move her. Her leg might fall off if I try to move her.

Following the emergency vet's instructions, I put my hands under her hindquarters and pull her very gently on to a rug. In which I wrap her, put her on the back seat of my car and, going very slowly, with the A-Z open on my lap, drive to the emergency clinic.

'There's really no point in your staying.'

'There's really no point in my going home. I wouldn't be able to sleep.'

'Okay,' he says, after a moment's hesitation. 'Try to make yourself comfortable out here.' He indicates the waiting room benches. I stretch myself out and put a pile of veterinary journals under my head. The fluorescent lights flicker overhead.

Have you ever waited while someone close to you has an operation? We don't do it, do we? We go home and after a time we telephone the nurses' station to hear that the patient is out of danger, or comfortable, or whatever euphemism comes to hand. So I have no idea how much time has passed before his voice filters through again:

'I think we've been able to save the leg.'

'Thank God.'

'You're very lucky. It was touch and go. The whole thing was touch and go.'

'I know. 'I'm immensely grateful to you. I don't think I've ever been more grateful to anyone. She's not my cat, you see.'

I tell my editor that I shall have to take a few days unpaid leave to nurse Samantha when she comes home. Naturally I am the laughing stock of the office. 'But she's not my cat,' I say in self-defence.

'And he calls that logic?'

Samantha is unusually docile and compliant when I take her home. She is wearing a strange lampshade thing round her neck to prevent her pulling at the stitches. Her face seems very small. She has difficulty in eating, with the weight of the lampshade on her neck, and to my astonishment takes her food from me, off a plastic spoon. Her milk I hold up for her in a Chinese coffee cup, tilting it towards her tongue. On her first night, she stands by my bed, asking to be lifted up. And there she sleeps. I make a little nest of pullovers for her, formed on one side into a low ridge, so that she can rest her neck. She stands up and miaows quietly when she wants to be let out.

Mrs. Graebner has been alerted to the recent drama. She has sent a bunch of flowers for the patient's bedside. She hopes to be home in a few days, to oversee the latter stages of the recovery. 'Or she will become dependent on poor Mr. Harris. She will never leave him.'

She leaves me all right. She hears the taxi before I do, the black tips of her ears twitching at the unfamiliar sound. Mrs. Graebner's rough, guttural voice has her up and walking unsteadily to the door. She stands behind it expectantly. 'All right, cat. Hang on. I'll take you up in a minute.'

I collect her bits and pieces, the pullovers in which she has been sleeping on my bed, the spoon from which I have been feeding her. She limps slowly behind me up to Mrs. Graebner's flat, her right leg held out stiffly, scarcely touching the ground.

Mrs. Graebner is standing in the doorway, her arms spread out in welcome. 'Sammy! My little Sammy! Who is Mama's little wounded soldier?' Samantha walks slowly past her into the flat, miserable in her lampshade. Tomorrow the vet will take it off.

'Mr. Harris. How can I ever thank you. You saved her life, you know.'

'Oh no. The vet saved her life.'

'With your help, Mr. Harris. Without you, she would be dead. I would like you to have this little gift . No, please. I insist. It was my husband's favourite.' She pushes a small object, wrapped in newspaper, into my hand. 'Is only a small thing. I would like to be able to let you have my Samantha, Mr. Harris. But you know I could never part with her.'

'I wouldn't take her, Mrs. Graebner. She's more trouble than she's worth.'

'You are a very naughty man, Mr. Harris. You love to tease, God bless you.'

She stands at her door as I make my way downstairs. The wretched cat has taken two weeks out of my life. For what? In my hand, the newspaper parcel springs suddenly to life. A violent rhythm is being beaten out on a little tin drum. The paper is beginning to tear.

'So sorry, Mr. Harris. Mr. Graebner, he was always going to mend.'

STELLA'S FRIENDS

A doting husband had persuaded her that she was attractive, so that when he died, in his sixties and her fifties, Stella had every expectation of re-marriage. After all, had not she been the one to shine, whilst George talked business and drank a little too enthusiastically either for sparkle or coherence? As the wife of a director of a multi-national company she had travelled widely and entertained freely. So now it's pay-back time, she thought. And waited for the invitations to roll in.

And they did. To coffee mornings, to bridge afternoons, to charity bazaars. Yes, her friends kept her in mind, but when it came to dinner parties they tended to excuse themselves.

'So loud.' 'Unpredictable.' 'Such a flirt.' 'I know I ought to ask her but...'

'George's death will have quietened her down a bit.' The husbands sounded reasonable. 'We ought to ask her, for his sake.'

But somehow she did not get asked. There was always some little reason why it was not appropriate to invite her. They tell you this is what happens. They tell you to expect it. But somehow she had not believed it, not of her own circle.

George died in November. In February Stella took herself off on a Caribbean cruise. It was like the Titanic, she thought. Drowning in widows. She was depressed by their number, still more depressed by the young crew staff trained to serve, listen, flatter and dance. Yes, it was fun to dance with young men - and they were good dancers - fun to flirt, but not even she could take them over the line beyond which they had been trained not to go. It wasn't worth their jobs. There were couples on board, and they were kind, and some husbands were allowed to dance with her. But then, they were never going to see her again. She thought, when she got home, that she would approach a dating agency. It might be fruitless, it might be dangerous - she had never minded danger - but it would be honest.

'I'm afraid it's still too soon.'

'Too soon for what?'

'Too soon after your husband's death. A year is recommended. We have found six months to be the very minimum.'

'Minimum?'

'Until six months have elapsed, we don't feel it is possible for a widow or widower to consider entering into what may turn out to be a long-term relationship. They are not ready.'

'I feel quite ready.'

'Perhaps, but we have taken professional advice on this, from psychologists and grief counsellors. And we must consider the men to whom you will be introduced. We have to be fair to all our clients.'

'I might miss a good one.'

'We have plenty of suitable partners for you on our books, I assure you. I do advise you to wait.'

'I'm sure I could find somewhere that would take me on.'

'I'm sure you could, Mrs. Masterson. But not, I venture to suggest, a reputable introduction agency.'

In April, Tim and Lorraine Cooper sent out invitations. The Coopers were on the fringes of the social set which had embraced George and Stella. Tim Cooper had not yet made it on to the board, and was probably unlikely to, although he had had some important postings and was well liked. The occasion was a fork supper, nothing fancy, come as you are. Just a chance for old friends to get together. And (to everyone except Stella) to catch up with Stella.

She telephoned her acceptance. 'But don't expect me to come as I am. Not unless you want me in bra and knickers.'

'Stella,' Lorraine said. 'She hasn't changed.'

She wore a tight, slinky number, long-sleeved but with the back cut out, and strappy, high-heeled shoes. She was overweight, but heroically resisted a size sixteen. 'Glamour puss,' George would have said, patting her bottom. 'Poor Stella' was the last image she wished to project.

Nevertheless. 'Poor Stella,' Lorraine said, greeting her. She put an arm round her shoulders and began to lead her into the room. 'Tim. Take Stella's coat and get her a drink while I take her over to the others.'

'I'm not ill,' Stella said.

'Of course not, dear. I just wanted to make it easier for you, the first time. You know.'

'It's not my fault it's the first time.'

'White wine, Stella?' Tim was coming across with a glass.

'I'd rather have gin, if you have any.'

'Of course,' he said, with no sign of irritation.

'Girls. Stella's here. Isn't that lovely.'

The group breaks apart to let her in. Voices lower and conversations peter out. Heads tilt to one side, held at an angle, awkward, quizzical. Odd that compassion should present like this, like a question mark.

'Stella. Dear.' Long, thin fingers, the nails carefully polished, are laid across her wrist. 'How are you? How have you been, dear, since George...'

'Since George died? Fair to bloody, if you really want to know.'

'I'm so sorry. It's been so awful for you. We've all missed you. We've been wanting to see you. We've been wanting to ask you round to dinner, trying to find the right ...'

Stella raises her eyebrows.

'Anyway it's lovely to see you now. And looking so *well*.' The speaker steps back and looks at her appreciatively. Stella's blonde hair has been carefully highlighted. She has a pale, underwater complexion which ages well.

'I'm not ill,' Stella says again.

'Of course not. But, you know, with what you've been through ...'

The little group of women murmurs assent. One might almost mistake it for warmth.

'How have you been coping?' The party has disseminated into smaller groups. She is buttonholed.

'I've had a lot to do. Solicitors. Probate. Contacting George's son.'

'He hasn't been difficult?'

'Not at all. I haven't seen him since the funeral.'

'Oh, shocking. Don't you find that shocking?'

'Not particularly. He never liked me. Why should that change because his father's dead?'

'No but surely, in common decency. I mean, he could have ...'

'A lot of people could have.'

The wives glance towards the safe haven of their husbands' sides.

'In February,' Stella is saying, 'In February, I went on a cruise.'

'A cruise? Wasn't that a bit ...'

'Soon? Wasn't that a bit soon, are you thinking? I don't know. I can't say. The thing is,' she raises her voice and throws back her head a little. The men have stopped talking and turned to look at her. 'The thing is, I'm looking for a husband. To fill the gap that George has left.'

'Oh but surely. I mean, it hasn't been very ...'

'Long. No, it hasn't been very long. Four months. Four months and five days, to be exact. But I don't see what time has to do with it. I like husbands. I like having one. I don't like being without one. I can't think what George was thinking of, popping off like that and leaving me husbandless.'

'Worn out,' one of the men says quietly.

'It was inconsiderate of him, to say the least, though I can't think he meant it. He always liked me to have what I wanted.' She has centre stage now. 'Any husbands on offer? Any of you had enough of your husbands? Because I'm in the market for one. Second-hand, second-rate, I'm not fussy.' She raises her glass towards the men and finishes brassily, 'God, I could use a husband!'

The men laugh uneasily, the women exchange glances.

'Stella is outrageous. I mean, it was all very well when George was alive, he encouraged this sort of behaviour, he basked in it. But now that she's a widow ...'

'Widow? Did I hear widow? What a deeply unpleasant word that is. A mean, pinched, narrow word. I don't like it. It doesn't sound like me.'

'It isn't you, dear. It's what's *happened* to you.'

The women incline gratefully towards a conversation they can handle. The men resume their gossip, glancing nervously at clocks and watches. There is a lot of evening left.

Presently Lorraine rings a little bell and invites them to come and help themselves to food. Don't hold back. There's plenty more where that came from.

The men follow the ladies into the dining-room.

'Poor old George. What he went through.'

'Oh, he loved it. Thrived on it.'

'I didn't know he had a son.'

'Oh yes. And a wife. Two, in fact, counting Stella.'

'I'm not with you.'

'He never got a divorce from his first wife. She wouldn't give him one and he wouldn't push for it. Stella took him on knowing that. Brave of her, if you think of it, at the time.'

'No-one would think twice about it today.'

'No. But thirty years ago...'

Lorraine is beside Stella at the dining table. 'Good to see you haven't lost your old sparkle, dear. George would have been proud of you. And Stella,' she lays a hand on her arm, 'things will look up, you know. There must be another George out there for you somewhere.'

Stella shrugs her shoulders, turns to the cold buffet. She stabs a salmon mousse with a fork. 'Oh bugger George,' she says.

THE BEACH HUT

Mrs Faye Harding dies in hospital in Peterborough, leaving the bulk of her estate to the Royal Society for the Protection of Birds, and her beach hut to Hilary Proctor, a woman she hardly knew.

'I think I'll take up hospital visiting,' Miss Proctor's friend Marilyn says, 'if beach huts drop out of the sky. Was she a bit ... you know?'

'No. She was quite sane.'

'Why you?'

'I don't know. Except that she had no children, and her nieces and nephews live abroad.'

'Still, it's a weird thing to do. Where is it anyway, this beach hut?'

Miss Proctor has no idea.

'Northumberland,' Mrs. Harding's solicitor says, lifting his head from a pile of papers. 'Low Winterton, north of Alnmouth. Beach Hut Number Twelve.'

'And the deeds?'

'No deeds.' He hands her a copy of Mrs. Harding's Will and a Bill of Sale dated 1975 when ownership of Hut Number Twelve passed from a Henry Lawson to George O'Hanlon, Mrs. Harding's father, for the sum of eighty pounds.

'I expect it's worth a lot more now,' Miss Proctor says. She pictures beach huts she has seen in the property pages, in places like the Isle of Wight, going for upwards of thirty thousand. Smart, tidy, second homes almost, brightly painted in blues, greens and yellows.

'Or less,' Mrs. Harding's solicitor says.

Miss Proctor re-directs her memory to other, actual huts she has seen, up on the coast at Cromer, paint peeling, roofs lifting, doors hanging open or missing altogether. Abandoned by owners waiting for the erosion of the cliffs to take them into the sea.

'How long since anyone used it?'

'Oh years, I should think. It was where Mrs. Harding's family spent their holidays when she was a girl. She did say that she loved it, that her happiest summers were spent there. I should sell it, if it's still there. Get a local agent on to it. It should have a site value, if nothing else.'

'I don't know,' Miss Proctor says. 'I've no idea what to do with it. But I should at least go and look at it. I think she meant me to.'

'Off on holiday already, Miss Proctor?'

'Yes, Mr. Mulholland. Just one week. It's in the Planner.'

'Ah yes. Though I think you usually go later in the year.'

'I do.' Miss Proctor generally takes her holiday from Mulholland and Atkinson's opticians, where she works as a receptionist, in August.

'Majorca again?'

'No. Northumberland this time.'

'Good gracious. That's a change. Well, when you come back ...'

'Yes?'

'When you come back, Miss Proctor ...'

'Yes, Mr. Mulholland?' Miss Proctor closes down her computer and looks at him.

'Never mind. It will keep. Have a very good holiday, Miss Proctor.'

Mr. Mulholland adjusts his half-moon spectacles and retires to his consulting room. Hilary Proctor sighs. Since his wife died, Mr. Mulholland has, on several occasions, been on the point of inviting her out. She feels sure of it. Hilary Proctor, good-looking, good-humoured, steady, on the wrong side of forty and without a man, has decided that Mr. Mulholland is her best chance. If only he could get past the point.

Miss Proctor takes the train from Peterborough, changing at York. The bleak sweeps of moorland and wild coastline of the border country appeal to her. From Alnmouth a taxi takes her to Low Winterton, a village of grey stone fishermen's cottages, set back from the sea behind a golf course and ridges of dunes. The Crown and Anchor, where the taxi puts her down, stands in the central square. Miss Proctor books in, goes up to her room, changes her shoes and hurries down to the beach.

It is late June, late afternoon. Children's cries reach her before she has arrived at the first line of dunes. Higher ridges, behind the first, lead on to the beach, or so she imagines as, slipping and chattering, families struggle back over them, trailing windbreaks and shrimping nets, cricket bats and buckets. Between the banks of dunes, in a long valley where she now stands and to which the families are returning, are the beach huts, a row of about fifteen.

They do not, at first glance, resemble the smart huts of the property section, although most have once been painted in bright colours. Others are plain wood, like garden sheds. All show signs of current, if not present occupation, with pairs of beach shoes lined up outside, and towels laid out to dry. All except one.

Number Twelve is derelict. It sits low in the sand, its felt roofing buckled, its blue paint faded and peeling, though some attempt appears to have been made, probably years ago, at reparation. In confirmation an ancient tin of paint lies outside the hut, rusting into the grass. Like a ship going down, Number Twelve lists a little to the west.

Miss Proctor has had no experience of family holidays and so surprises herself by a desire to cry. Crying for what? She takes a breath, steps cautiously on to the wooden platform and tries the door. It is locked. Her hut. Who has locked it? Who has the right? Miss Proctor, unreasonable in her disappointment, blames everyone but herself for failing to obtain that most essential of accessories to a new property – the key.

At the Crown and Anchor she is told there is a lad called Robbie Borthwick knows about those beach huts. Lives at Castle Cottages, number six.

A tall, slightly-built man in his late fifties is standing on a ladder burning the paint off a window frame. His blue workman's overalls are spattered with white paint. Flakes are in his greying hair, on his hands, and, when she reaches the ladder and looks up at him, his face. She waits for a pause:

'Excuse me. Castle Cottages?"

He nods.

'Number six?'

'Yes.'

'Is your son in?'

'I haven't got a son.

'Robbie Borthwick?'

'That's me.'

'Oh. Oh I see.' Robbie. Lad. The words had suggested someone younger.

'You wanted something?'

'I have a beach hut here. But I haven't got a key and it's locked. I was hoping you'd be able to help me.'

He looks at her. 'You have a beach hut?'

'Yes.'

'They're privately owned, those huts. I know all the owners. I don't know you.'

'I was left it. In a Will. A lady called Mrs. Harding left it to me.'

'Mrs. Harding's dead?'

'Yes.'

'Ah,' he says. He sets his blow-torch carefully on the window-sill. 'I'd better come down,' he says.

He won't come that day, he is too busy. Sundays he goes to dinner with his niece. Monday he has a job over at Alnwick. It might be finished Monday, it might not. He could probably get along Tuesday afternoon, round about …'

'What time did you say?' She struggles to hear his unfamiliar accent, pitched somewhere between Geordie and lowland Scots.

'Ah said, foor.'

'Oh, four. Right. I'll meet you there. It's number twelve.'

'I know the hut,' he says.

Tuesday is raw and windy. She has walked twice out on to the beach and back again when she sees him coming. He wears his blue overalls. In one hand he carries a toolbox and a bunch of keys.

'I didn't know you had the key.'

'I don't know that I do have the key. I have keys. One may fit.'

He bends down and inspects the lock. Out of his box he takes a can of oil and sprays it into the keyhole, wiping it carefully with a rag. 'Years since it's been turned,' he says. He tries one key after another. Nothing. Finally he takes the tools out of his box and fishes around in the bottom.

'Got a few loose ones,' he says. 'You never know.'

The second key slips easily into the lock and he turns the knob. The door opens with difficulty, creaking against the hinges, and jams half way. He puts his head round the door and peers inside. 'Welcome to Number Twelve,' he says.

She moves to go in.

'No. Let me. The floorboards will be rotten.'

He eases inside, feeling the boards with each step. Several give way. He beckons her in, indicating where she should place her feet.

Inside, the hut is empty. Spiders' webs hang across the roof and in the corners. Mouse droppings lie among sand on the floor. Marram grass has forced its way through gaps in the wood and some has taken root. A narrow bench runs round the inside walls. Mouse droppings are here too, and yellow sticky balls of spiders' nests.

'Funny,' she says. 'I expected to find stuff in here. Shrimping nets. Kettles. Signs of a life.'

'Oh no. They always cleared it out at the end of summer.'

'They?'

'The O'Hanlons. Mrs. Harding's family.'

'I wonder what I should do,' she says, lowering herself to sit on the bench.

'Not that, for a start.' He pulls her roughly back by the arm. He puts out his hand and presses on the bench. A piece splits off. He tears it to pieces and lets them fall to the floor.

'Wood's rotten, he says. 'Wet from the sand. It's blown up and drifted against the sides. And under the floorboards. That's why the marram's coming through.'

'I thought sand was dry,' she says.

'And how would grass grow in it?' He looks at her. 'A lot you know.'

'It doesn't look too bad from the outside,' she says.

'That's the paint. It hides the true condition of the wood. You can't tell what it's like under the paint. But they all want their beach huts painted, don't they.'

They close up the hut and walk back over the golf course towards the village. A white van, *R.A. Borthwick, Carpenter and Joiner* painted on the side, is parked in the square.

'You'll be selling, won't you?'

'In that condition?'

'No, not in that condition. You'll have to spend some money on it, but not as much as if you wanted a proper job.'

'What would that cost me, a proper job?'

'A thousand, maybe more.'

'That's a lot.'

'Well, you won't do it, will you. You'll go back to London and decide it's not worth it.'

'I'm not from London.'

'Aren't you? You're not from up here.'

'No.'

'I didn't think so. There's nowhere like up here.' He slides back the door of his van.

'Will you give me a couple of estimates, one for a proper job, one for a patch-up job.'

'I'm not mucking about doing estimates for nothing. I don't need the work. You let me know when you've decided.' He starts up the engine and drives away.

'Did you enjoy your holiday, Miss Proctor?'

'Very much, Mr. Mulholland, thank you.' Miss Proctor has walked and bird-watched. In the evenings she has sat by her beach hut and leant against it, listening to the sea. She has taken a boat to the Farne Islands. The O'Hanlons would have done that, and laughed at the puffins with their sudden, splashy landings and bills like brightly painted beach huts.

'And how was Northumberland?'

'Very beautiful. Remote. Not what I was expecting, but then I don't quite know what I was ...'

'Quite so. Thank you, Miss Proctor. Would you show Mr. Thornton in please?'

Miss Proctor finds Mr. Borthwick's telephone number and tells him she would like an estimate for the proper job. He says he supposes she knows what she's doing. He says it's a fair weather job and whatever happens he won't be able to start on it till the Spring. He has a lot of other jobs on the go. He doesn't need the work.

Mr. Borthwick's estimate, e-mailed to her office, is not the clearest document Miss Proctor has ever received. Nevertheless she struggles through it and concludes that the figure is probably justified.

'You're not accepting it?' her friends are horrified. 'It's over a thousand pounds.'

'It needs a lot doing to it.'

'But what *for?*'

Miss Proctor lives in rented accommodation. The beach hut is the first property she has ever owned. 'I liked it up there.'

'But a beach hut! What use to you is a beach hut?' And where, they add, does she think she is going to find the money.

Miss Proctor gives Mr. Borthwick the go-ahead.

'Miss Proctor?'

'Yes, Mr. Mulholland.'

'Would you check the Optikaladvances.uk website please. Mrs. Fletcher has seen some vari-focals she would like to try.

'Certainly Mr. Mulholland.'

At the same time, she checks her e-mail.

Tuesday, 28th October 2004, 10.36 AM

From: raborthwick@openworld.com

To: hilaryproctor.mulholatkinson@btconnect.com

Subject: Hut

Hut to be raised minimum one and a half meters. Should be done before winter and easterlies. Requirements: four railway sleepers @ ten pounds each; three men for two days @ one hundred pounds per person per day. Additional expenditure six hundred and forty pounds. Please okay.

R. Borthwick

Miss Proctor okays, and cancels Majorca for another year.

In November Miss Proctor thinks she should take a look at the expensively raised hut and books a Saturday night at the Crown and Anchor. It is dusk when she arrives but she takes a torch and walks over the golf course to the beach. Her hut stands proudly above the sand, no longer leaning. She climbs over the dunes and on to the beach. Groups of waders run backwards and forwards along the water's edge. She watches them until the light has gone.

The following day Robbie Borthwick joins her at the hut. He won't be doing any more work on it this year, but at least it's off the ground now, and won't get any worse. In the Spring he will see what can be done with the wet timbers. Some will need replacing. Some might dry out enough to be given a coat of preservative. At this stage he can't tell. Miss Proctor settles with him for work done to date.

Mr. Mulholland asks Miss Proctor if she will organise the staff Christmas party again this year. He thinks that the dinner at the Kon Tiki last year went very well. Unfortunately he will not be able to attend himself as he is going to stay with his late wife's sister in Portishead.

Tuesday, 8 March 2005, 15.35 PM

From: raborthwick@btopenworld.com

To: hilaryproctor.mulholatkinson@btconnect.com

Subject: Hut

Need to replace most of floor area. Timbers rotten.

Additional expenditure one

hundred and sixty pounds. Please okay.

R. Borthwick

Miss Proctor has planned a Spring City Break in Prague with her friend Marilyn. She explains, over a pizza, that she really can't do it this year. Maybe next year, when her finances are more sorted.

'It's that hut, isn't it? It's taking up all your time and money. I just hope it's not money down the drain.'

Wednesday, 13 April 2005, 10.43 AM

From: raborthwick@btopenworld.com

To: hilaryproctor.mulholatkinson@btconnect.com

Subject: Hut

Floor finished. Wall timbers drying out. Did you want a

verandah?

R. Borthwick

A verandah. Miss Proctor finds the original estimate and searches through it. No mention of a verandah. But a verandah would be fine, wouldn't it. A verandah would be the icing on the cake. A yellow beach hut with a white verandah. Like in the property pages. Additional expenditure? No mention. Still, now that it is in her imagination, it cannot not be realised.

She meets Robbie Borthwick in the bar of the Crown and Anchor. He's had his tea, but takes a pint of bitter with her while she eats scampi and chips.

'Here, I'll draw it for you.' He puts down his glass and gets out a pad and pencil. 'It's like a balustrade. I'd join it at the sides and run it all the way round the platform leaving a gap in front of the door. It would look nice.'

'Additional expenditure?'

'Oh not much. I've got some banisters I could use. Say sixty pounds.'

'Did there used to be one?'

'Yes. Yes, there did. We used to throw our wet towels over it when we came out of the sea.'

'We?'

'The O'Hanlons and my brother and me. Once they were here for the summer we spent all our time with them.'

'You liked her, Mrs. Harding?'

His blue eyes meet her enquiry. 'I did.'

'A lot?'

'Oh it's no good thinking about things like that. She was always going to go off and marry someone like an army officer. I knew that.'

For reasons of health Mr. Mulholland's partner, Mr. Atkinson, has decided to take early retirement. His replacement will not be available for several weeks. Mr. Mulholland asks Miss Proctor whether she would mind, for a short spell, staying on an extra hour or so occasionally to help clear the backlog. He will see that she is reimbursed.

'Of course not, Mr. Mulholland.'

Miss Proctor has not anticipated such a falling-out over the creosote. As soon as she receives the e-mail informing her that the verandah is finished and Mr. Borthwick is going to burn off all the existing paint and apply three coats of creosote she is on the telephone.

'I don't want it creosoted. I want it painted.'

'Creosote's best. Paint peels. Begins to flake off after six months.'

'I hate creosote. It smells. Like a garden shed.'

'Garden sheds last.'

'I don't want a garden shed. I want a beach hut. A painted beach hut. I am the client.'

'Well you'll be a client without an employee. Because I'm not doing it.'

'That brought you up quick smart,' he says. He is waiting for her in the bar.

'We've got to get something sorted out. I can't have creosote, Robbie, I just can't. A yellow beach hut with a white verandah. That's what's in my mind.'

'It's not sensible. It's a waste of your money.'

'It's my money.'

'What are you, an heiress or something?'

She flushes. 'You know I'm not.'

'So how did you get to know someone like Mrs. Harding?'

'I used to visit her in hospital. I liked her. I think she liked me. Her sight was bad. I read the newspapers to her, chatted about current affairs.'

'She didn't talk about her childhood?'

'Only to say it had been happy. She used to say old people are crashing bores, all they ever do is reminisce.'

'She never mentioned me?'

'No. Her death was a shock. She can't have been very old.'

'She wasn't. Funny she should leave the hut to you.'

'Yes. Though she had no children and her husband had died.'

'Funny, all the same.' He looks at her. 'I expect she knew what she was doing.'

'So where are we with the creosote?' A silence has settled between them, though nothing has been resolved.

'I've told you. Painting is a waste of your money.'

'Well such money as I have I'll spend as I like. I choose to spend it on having the hut painted, and I hope you will agree to do it. If not, I'll have to find someone else. And if that means additional expenditure, so be it.'

'It's still got to be stripped,' he says.

'Okay.'

'It will cost more.'

'Okay.'

'It'll take much longer.'

'So the sooner it's started, the sooner it's finished. I'll help you. I've got an extra day. Come on, we'll start first thing.'

'You're a hard woman,' he says.

She is there before him, waiting in the early morning sun in her jeans, an old shirt, and a cotton headscarf tied over her hair. When he sees her he smiles.

'Who'd have thought it,' he says.

He shows her how to hold the blowtorch, scraping off the crinkled, peeling paint himself as it bubbles under the heat. He says it's easier with two, you can get the paint off before it has time to cool. It lies in blue curls on the sand around them.

At midday they stop for sandwiches and the coffee Miss Proctor has brought in a thermos flask.

'Coffee,' he says. He holds the beaker at arm's length. 'Up here we drink tea.'

'Drink it and be grateful. It's not every day you get an assistant.'

By early evening a wind has got up. Miss Proctor is pleased she has had the foresight to take an extra day off. By now she would have missed the train to Peterborough. Despite the blowtorch, she is cold, and blisters are beginning to appear on her fingers. She pulls away and looks at them.

'Are you spoken for, Miss Proctor?'

She looks at him, startled. 'That's a funny phrase.' Then, quickly, 'Hilary, please.'

'Are you spoken for?' he repeats.

'No. No, not really.'

'Then I would not be out of turn in asking you to take a bite with me when we've finished.'

'No. Not at all.'

'We'll drive up the coast,' he says. 'There's terns nesting at Beadnell Bay. I'll show you.'

She sits in the front of his van and waits. He places his tools and blowtorch in the back, takes off his overalls, folds them carefully and lays them on top. He puts on a jacket which has lain across the back of the seat, dusting off the shoulders with the back of his hand. As he gets into the driver's seat he glances in the onside mirror and smoothes his hair.

'A bit more respectable,' he says.

Later, he drives her back to the Crown and Anchor. He slides back the door and hands her down. His skin is rough.

'Was your father a carpenter?' she says.

'No. Fisherman. When the living went out of it he went down to Craster. Worked in the smokehouses.'

'Smoking what?'

'Herrings.' He looks at her. 'You've never heard of Craster kippers?'

'No.'

'Never had one?'

'No.'

'That's something we'll have to put right.'

'Miss Proctor.'

'Yes, Mr. Mulholland.' Miss Proctor is hesitating about closing down her computer. She is wondering, Mr. Atkinson's replacement due to arrive on Monday, whether she will be required to stay an extra hour.

'Miss Proctor, I am most grateful for all the extra work you have put in recently.'

'Not at all, Mr. Mulholland.'

'In view of which, Miss Proctor ...'

'Yes, Mr. Mulholland?'

'In view of which ...' Mr. Mulholland removes his spectacles, blows on the lenses and begins to polish vigorously with his handkerchief, 'in view of which I was wondering, Miss Proctor, if you would do me the honour of ... er... of joining me for dinner tomorrow evening.'

Miss Proctor looks at him, intent on his polishing. Out of the corner of her eye she sees that a message has come up on her screen. She glances at it.

> Friday, 20 May 2005, 15.45 PM
> From: raborthwick@btopenworld.com
> To: hilaryproctor.mulholatkinson@btconnect.com
> Subject: Hut
> Undercoat finished. Planning to start the topcoat Monday.
> Robbie

Well. She will need to go up to choose the yellow paint.